Living
Suspended Lives

A Dark Journey

The Sequel to
Trouble at Our Door

KIRK STEWART

PAGE PUBLISHING, INC.
New York, NY

First originally published by Page Publishing, Inc. 2017

ISBN 978-1-64082-907-7 (Paperback)
ISBN 978-1-64082-908-4 (Digital)

Printed in the United States of America

This book is dedicated to all those who experienced the dark journey of our suspended lives with us. It includes my brother and his wife and, of course, our children and grandchildren. It is also dedicated to my pastor and his wife, who faithfully edited the book for me.

I want to especially dedicate it to our parents, none of whom lived to see the work completed. It is also in memory of all the friends and family we lost during our dark journey.

Preface

Kara Phillip (my wife) and myself (Jack Phillips) were sentenced for the crime of manufacturing methamphetamine and related charges in August of 1998 and sentenced on December 5, 1998. We were tried and sentenced at the Clifford Davis Federal Building in the federal court of the Western District of Tennessee by the Honorable Judge Jason T. Burns. Kara received a sentence of 168 months. I received a sentence of 262 months.

Our story—the events of the crime, our trial, and our sentencing—were all told in the first book of the series, *Trouble at Our Door*. That book covered all the occurrences involved in the above-mentioned events and told how our lives were turned upside down. That book ended just after our sentences had been imposed. The following is from that first book:

> The U.S. Marshalls handcuffed us and led us out of the courtroom. We were taken to the elevators and then to another floor in the building. I don't know for sure if we went up or down. It didn't matter much now. What did matter was Kara. We ignored the Marshals and talked and kissed and told each other how much we loved the other one, and we both tried to encourage each other.
>
> When we got off the elevator we turned right down a short hallway. There were offices with doors of halfglass on each side of the hallway. We were taken into an office on the right

side. It had a long counter (as did the office across the hallway) like you might see at a Department of Motor Vehicle Office. The Marshalls told us to say good bye. I told them that our attorney was coming, but they just looked at me blankly.

We told each other good bye. I kissed Kara and looked her in the eyes and said, "Stay strong Kara and live through this. We'll do what we can to get out."

Kara shook her head as tears streamed down her face and she said, "I love you, Jack," Just like she had said to me a million times before. It had never meant so much!

I told her, "I love you, too, Kara."

One of the Marshalls took her by the right elbow and walked to and through the door, across the hallway, and through the door on the other side. They continued walking the length of the long counter in that office. I kept watching and hoping Kara would tum around so I could see her face one more time. She never turned around. I watched her walking away from me until she reached the end of the counter, and then they turned left and were gone. It was December 5, 1998. I wondered if I would ever see Kara, my wife, again. I felt like the death angel had passed between us.

Our story continues in this book, *Living Suspended Lives*. You are invited to live this with us. It is personal, heartbreaking, triumphant, sad, and emotional.

Chapter 1

December 5, 1998
Back to Mason for Me

Do not forget to entertain strangers, for by so doing some have unwittingly entertained angels. Remember the prisoners as if chained with them those who are mistreated-since you yourselves are in the body also.

—Hebrews 13:2,3, RKIV

Kara was gone. I stood perfectly still just staring at where I had last seen her. I couldn't believe she didn't turn around. I guess I expected her to reappear and look back at me. It didn't happen. The US Marshal seemed to be waiting, too. I actually thought, "He is giving her time to come back." Finally, he said, "Let's go, Phillips." I wasn't going to get to see her.

I couldn't speak. I turned around and let him lead me back to the hallway where the holding cells were. He opened the door, and we walked in. Keith Hawkins was in the first cell, and no one was in the second cell. The Marshal put me into the cell with Keith. I asked him where the other men were that had ridden over there with us. He told me they had all gone back except one man. He said he had gone into court about an hour ago.

I sat down and related the sentences we had been given. Keith felt almost as badly as I did. I know he was really hurting for me.

He felt like I was family and had been mistreated. He was probably more angry than me at the moment. I wasn't all tied up about the length of sentence I had received. I was all hung up on the sentence Kara had received. Reality hit me again that I might not see her again for twenty years, if at all. I had already felt like I had died with all that had been lost. I wasn't worried about doing the time. I really just didn't care. It was Kara I was concerned about. How would (or could) she possibly do fourteen years?

No one knew her better than me. I knew how strong she really was, and I knew her inner strength. I knew she was a tough, strong person despite her apparently being a docile person outwardly. Everyone had always assumed we had a one-sided relationship. It was perceived that I was the dominant partner, almost dictatorial, and that she was merely passive. They were all wrong. You can't sustain a relationship or marriage with that structure. We had a cooperative relationship. She never allowed me to bulldozer her. There really was give and take in every area. She stood her ground frequently and won her share of our disagreements and arguments.

I was primarily concerned about the time she was sentenced to serve. She was forty-five. With the length of her sentence, she would be almost sixty when she would be released. I also knew there were no federal prisons for women nearby. That meant she would be virtually isolated from family and friends. She would certainly be alone. That was reason enough for me to be worried about her.

Then in the next minute my own situation would flood back over me and almost consume me. I felt as if I were literally going to be *buried* under the 262-month sentence I had been given. I would be close to seventy if I survived it. I felt like my life was already over. All my hopes and dreams and aspirations were gone. There was only a blank slate. Keith tried to provide some comfort for me. He kept trying to encourage me by telling me I still had plenty of chances left and that I needed to keep fighting.

Finally, the other inmate returned from court. It was 5:45 p.m. We were all shackled up and led to the elevators and then down below to the parking garage. We waited for a few minutes and then the van showed up. We were placed in the back of the van and locked in. Keith and I sat on the left side, and the other inmate, Roger McKnight, sat on the right side.

McKnight told us he was locked up for threatening to kill then-president Clinton. He said he was in court that day to determine if he was mentally capable to stand trial. The judge had already ordered his psychological evaluation and now was setting a date for a preliminary hearing to discuss the results of that evaluation.

I realized it was going to be after 6:30 p.m. before we made it back to Mason. Just as we hit I-40 East, the interstate that would take us to the Mason exit, the van exited at Sycamore View. This was the first exit after you got on I-40 East toward Nashville. The officers told us we had to go by the Shelby County Penal Farm to pick up an inmate.

We drove to the facility and were allowed through the outer gate onto the prison grounds. One of the officers grabbed some paperwork and got out of the van. He was gone a long time. About 8:00 p.m., he and an inmate (handcuffed) came out of the facility a long distance from the van and began walking toward us. The other officer got out of the van and waited for them to make the long walk. He shackled up the man just like we were shackled. The inmate had all his possessions in a large black garbage bag. The officer just threw that in the back with all of us and placed the inmate in the back of the van next to Roger.

I was really surprised when Keith exchanged greetings. Keith said, "Steve, how you doin', man?"

Steve replied, "Fine, Keith, now that I am out of that dump." Keith introduced Steve to Roger and me.

Steve was in for bank robbery. He was also originally from somewhere in Arkansas. His dad was a retired attorney. His mom and dad lived in a nice part of Memphis over near the Racquet Club. They had money and owned a very successful retail business. Steve had a college degree, had been married and divorced, and didn't seem like a criminal at all. He told Keith he had been sentenced to sixty months. He had just completed fifteen months at the Penal Farm on a state weapons charge. He was redheaded and told us everyone just called him Red.

Our van didn't reach Mason until about 8:50 p.m. By the time we were processed in, it was after 9:00 p.m. All four of us were headed to B-Pod, so we walked down the hall in single file against the right wall. As we entered B-Pod, Roger headed to his cell, and Red went off to find his new cell.

AC approached Keith and me as we entered, and he said, "Damn, Coach, it's so late we all thought you had won and gone home." I looked around, and almost all the men in the unit were standing around in groups of three or four just looking at us. I wondered if they had been waiting for us.

AC said, "Coach, how much time did you get?"

I told him, "I got 262 months, and Kara, my wife, got 168 months."

The look on his face almost matched the look I had seen just a little while earlier on Kara's face. Total shock. He just shook his head from side to side and turned and walked back toward the other men. He told them the sentences, and all at once, all the men just turned around and headed back to their individual cells. They went in and quietly closed the heavy metal doors, which locked automatically. It was eerily quiet. Keith and I just looked at each other. We returned to our cell and closed our door as well.

The next morning, I asked AC, "What was that all about last night? Why did you and all of the men just walk away, go in your cells and close the door?"

He said, "Coach, you' re a schoolteacher and a first-time offender. Most of us believe you are innocent. It's obvious to all of us you are not the criminal type. But we are all gangbangers. Most of us all have lengthy criminal records. We have been in and out of jail all our lives. If the feds gave you 262 months, what kind of chance do you think we have when we get sentenced? We just couldn't handle it, man! By the way, sorry they hammered your ass like they did."

Chapter 2

December 1998
Back at Mason

The Bible study group and prayer group I had started back in August following our conviction grew both in numbers and in importance. I found a real challenge in leading and teaching these groups. I also had a great opportunity. Everyone seemed to be watching me a little closer to see how I would handle the unbelievable sentences Kara and I had been given. I had to demonstrate that I really believed in and trusted God even when circumstances were so horrible. It was my greatest opportunity to demonstrate my faith was genuine. If I screwed this up, I might as well fold the Bible study and the prayer group. I would have no witness or standing in regard to religion with the men. I recalled the vow I had made after I was convicted, that I would serve God and be faithful no matter what happened and that I would not despair. That vow was not lightly made. I would trust God to fulfill his promise to me. He did.

I called home later the night we were sentenced. Kara had called Paul earlier and told him she was all right and would call the next night at 6:00 p.m. as usual. I was relieved that she had settled down, but I was so anxious to hear it from her myself. I could tell a lot just from the tone of her voice. That phone call actually encouraged me. It helped me to settle down and focus on trying to clear my own head to begin serving that time. After all, I already had served four months.

The Bible study, the prayer group, and the church became more and more important to me. It was my great solace in those days. Keith was also a comforting friend. I can't imagine how I could have coped without any one of those things.

As the weekend approached, I was anxious to see Paul and Jen. On Saturday, when we began talking, I realized they both seemed very upset. I tried to assure them that I would be fine. God's grace would somehow sustain me. We discussed a few other things, and Paul agreed to go see Lester Moore and try to get our appeal papers filed and a motion in for a new trial.

Of course we had the affidavits from the thirteen men at Mason. Some had already transferred, but we knew we could find them. We had found out that despite Nance and Tisdale denying they had deals at trial, they had both received Rule 35bs from the government. Both had their sentences substantially reduced by testifying against Kara and me. Nance got 48 months knocked off his sentence of 168 months in Missouri, and Tisdale got 34 months knocked off his 100 months sentence in Missouri. Phil Watson, our football player and attorney, had seen all that on his computer and contacted Paul. We had all been sure they had a deal despite what they said and what the AUSA had said at trial and sentencing. Now it was a proven fact. Also, we had always known they had immunity because they were never charged for the crime they admitted committing. We were also more sure than ever that Nance's and Tisdale's trial testimony had been craftily planned, practiced, rehearsed, and perfectly executed. They had given such contradictory statements prior to trial, which had been changed to fit the planned presentation. Terry Descusio (AUSA) and Mike March (DEA Agent) had coordinated the changes in testimony to fit their scenario of the crime to include Kara and me. The Assistant United States Attorney, Terry Descusio, had corrupted his office.

Chapter 3

Preparing for Christmas, 1998

This would be the first Christmas away from my family since 1951. I knew that would be difficult. The staff at CCA Mason put up a notice on our bulletin board that we would be allowed to have a twenty-five-pound Christmas box sent in. Of course, there were many items we could not have (and all boxes would be thoroughly searched), but the list of banned items was surprisingly short. There were all kinds of restrictions on those things that we could have; they had to be store-bought, still wrapped, and unopened, for example.

I began putting a list together. Nacho told me he would not be getting a box, so we made a deal. I would have my brother send a second twenty-five-pound box in his name, and we would split the goodies.

I saw an immediate opportunity to make some money as well. I took orders for cigarettes you couldn't buy on commissary and included those cartons of cigarettes as part of my orders. I sold each carton for a profit. I collected by having the other inmates purchase items from commissary for me. In some cases, I just gave them an order for goods to be shipped in their twenty-five-pound box. I was rolling in merchandise. I also had a lengthy IOU list for future collections. Business was good.

We also decorated for Christmas and bought cards and other specialty items at the commissary. We even had a Christmas tree in the unit and in the visiting room. However, it was still a very difficult time. I don't think I had ever been so lonely. I had heard my dad talk about being away from home during WWII. He never could hide the lonely feelings he had, and he didn't try to. I also realized how difficult our absence would be for the families back home.

Our families seemed almost paralyzed. They had a difficult time committing to Christmas. Mom and Dad were both in declining health. Mary Lynn and her family and our son, Carey, didn't have their heart in celebrating Christmas. After all, their mom and dad would not be there. Paul was totally lost, and Kara's family was going through the same thing.

I had never considered such a scenario. I found myself having to serve in the role as a comforter to our families and encourage them to enjoy the holiday even if we weren't going to be there. I had to keep a happy face at visits and an upbeat tone in my voice on the phone. There was no way I could let them know how depressed, lonely, and discouraged I really was.

When Kara and I had our nightly telephone talks, she cried a lot. I had to try to uplift her as well. I could not let her see or know that I was hurting just as much as she was. We were both struggling to cope. Missing that first Christmas still brings a sadness to me. About all we had were our phone calls and letters.

Chapter 4

On the Legal Front

I learned from Paul that Lester Moore had filed our motion for a new trial on December 14, 1998. He had also filed a motion stating our intention to appeal (as he had been directed by the judge to do). We hoped the motion for a new trial might actually lead to something positive.

Phillip Watson and Paul were hard at work trying to gather more evidence on our case. We really only had the thirteen affidavits, the inconsistent testimonies, and the Rule 35bs. We all felt we had some good grounds on Tisdale's statement that had appeared in our PSI considering the AUSA had claimed no such statement existed, and we went to trial empty-handed in regard to what Tisdale might testify about. By law, we were certainly entitled to that statement.

The two witnesses had also been rewarded for their testimony with sentence reductions and immunity from prosecutions. They had deals with the government. It was obvious they had lied about it under oath and that the AUSA had also lied and misrepresented the truth at trial and at sentencing. Those would be the issues that Lester Moore would surely include in his motion. June Riley had filed a motion to appeal on Kara's behalf as well, but not a motion for a new trial.

I had already paid Lester Moore twenty-five thousand dollars at this point. Mom and Dad had refinanced their home for that. Our family home had been paid for in full since 1977. Now all the equity had been squeezed out for my defense (but I lost at trial). I didn't know how we could pay for my appeal. I knew it would cost at least another ten thousand dollars. That was a real problem. My family didn't have that kind of cash. I was already sickened that we had paid the twenty-five thousand dollars.

One important thing Paul decided to do was to find R. A. Boone. If he really started the fire, why didn't he testify at trial? We knew the government could have found him if they wanted to. We suspected they did find him and that he had denied having anything to do with that fire, which resulted in the authorities finding the meth lab. After all, Nance and Tisdale had placed him at the scene and accused him of starting the fire while they slept. We surmised he must have denied those accusations and probably had an ironclad alibi as to where he really was. Otherwise, the authorities would have surely charged him or offered him immunity to testify against us.

On December 15, 1998, Paul decided to go to Southeast Missouri and look for R. A. Boone. He called Mom and Dad, who were back home in Rector, Arkansas, that week and told them what he was about to do. The thinking was that R. A. Boone might deny the testimony of Nance and Tisdale. That would be a nice piece of new evidence to have. Two hours after the call to Mom and Dad's, Paul was at their house. We had been told of a man in Portageville, Missouri, who had worked with RA at one time. Paul looked up his number in the phone book and called him and learned two things: first, R. A. Boone had lived at Caruthersville, Missouri, for quite a while at one time, and second, he didn't live there now but lived and worked at a factory near Campbell, Missouri. This man said RA had worked at the factory for at least five years. He said RA would be at work that day until about 4:30 p.m. He also told Paul that RA drove a red jeep. Paul asked the man if he would go with him to Campbell and identify RA. to him. The man agreed to go and Paul would pick him up at 3:30 p.m. in Portageville, Missouri.

Since it was still morning, Paul decided to drive over to Caruthersville to the police station and see what he could learn about R. A. Boone. When he got there, he saw that the Caruthersville Police Department and the Pemiscot County Sheriff's office were both housed in the same building.

Paul was in for a real surprise when he began questioning the authorities about R. A. Boone. He learned RA and his family had been firmly entrenched in Southeast Missouri for a long time. One of the deputies there told Paul that his own dad, who had been chief of police, was R. A. Boone's dad's best friend. He described RA as "a really good ole boy." He admitted RA had had a few run-ins with the law, but it was not serious, and RA had no criminal record. He told Paul he might want to talk to a retired officer who had served for over thirty years. Paul said he planned to talk to him.

That resulted in two really scary and strange occurrences. First, after Paul had told them about the case, the role of Nance and Tisdale, and how they had testified about RA, a detective asked Paul, "Are you armed?"

Paul said, "No."

He then asked Paul, "Do you have a gun in your car?"

Again, Paul replied, "No," but quickly added, "Do I need one?"

He told Paul, "You might if you keep asking the questions you are asking and talking about the people and things you are talking about."

Paul said all kinds of alarms went off. He found it all very bizarre. Could he be in danger to the point that he needed a gun to just ask a few questions about RA Boone (and/or Nance and Tisdale)? Should he even bother going to talk to Carroll Trail, the retired police officer who now lived about twenty miles away? As he was thinking about these things, the officer asked him, "Do you really want to talk to Carroll Trail?"

Paul replied, "Yes, I think I do."

The detective said, "Okay," then turned around at his desk and picked up the phone and obviously punched in an out-of-town phone number. While the phone was ringing, he turned to Paul and said, "What time are you going over there?"

Paul answered, "I would say sometime shortly after 6:30 p.m." Paul still had to pick up the man at Portageville and have him at Campbell, Missouri, at 4:30 p.m. to see and possibly talk to R. A. Boone.

When someone finally answered the officer's call, the officer said, "Carroll, there's a man here at the office who would like to talk to you about RA Boone."

There was a pause, then the detective turned and asked Paul to give him his name again. Paul told him, "Paul Phillips."

The officer relayed that over the phone and then added, "He's in his 50s, about 5 feet 8 inches tall, and about 185 pounds." He then looked out the window and added, "He's driving a red Camaro with Tennessee tags."

The detective paused and then said over the phone, "Okay, I will tell him."

He turned to Paul when he hung up the phone and said, "He said he would talk to you, but don't bring anybody with you."

Paul thought how weird the entire conversation was. He asked the detective if he could use his phone. The detective said, "Yeah, go ahead." All Paul could think about was letting Mom and Dad know where he was at that moment, where he was going later in the afternoon, what times he was going to be at various places, and what time they should expect him home. He told Mom he should be back at her house no later that 7:30 p.m. She told him to call home after he had checked out R. A. Boone and dropped the man off in Portageville, then to call when he was headed to Fraley, Missouri, to see Carroll Trail, and to call her from the Trail house as soon as he arrived there. She said, "The moment you leave his house, find a pay phone and call me and tell me exactly where you are." Before the conversation ended, she said, "Paul, call this all off if it gets too dangerous." He thought it was very near that point now. Was he being setup?

Paul did reach the factory where RA worked near Campbell, Missouri, before the 4:30 p.m. shift change. When the shift change occurred, the man from Portageville who was semihiding in the back seat pointed out R. A. Boone as soon as he stepped through the factory doors.

Paul was out of the car and shouting at RA, "Hey, RA, just a minute! I want to talk to you. Just a minute!" When RA looked at Paul, he bolted. He took off running as fast as he could and jumped into his red jeep and sped away. Paul said it was obvious that RA had been tipped by the authorities in Caruthersville that he was looking for him.

Paul went back to his car and attempted to follow RA. It ended up in a chase on gravel back roads outside of Campbell, Missouri, where Paul lost him. While driving around, he saw an old country store, the only store/gas station he had seen, so he stopped in. He asked the old gentleman running the little store, "Do you know R. A. Boone?"

The man said, "Sure, he stops in here every day."

Paul asked where RA lived, and the old man pointed down the road to the north of the store and said, "First house on the left. You can't miss it. It's the prefabricated house with a built-on front porch."

Paul drove down the road. There on the mailbox in bold letters was the name R. A. Boone. He had found the house in less than seven hours, including the time to drive from Memphis and the time he had spent in Caruthersville. As he drove, he was thinking that it was now clear that either the DEA had not looked for R. A. Boone like they said, or that they had looked and found him and discovered another lie that Nance and Tisdale had testified about. Either way, R. A. Boone bad not been difficult to find even for a schoolteacher from Memphis.

When Paul let the man off in Portageville, he called Mom from a pay phone. He still had one more stop. That would be at the Carroll Trail home in Fraley, Missouri. Paul was anxious to see what the retired police officer would have to say. He arrived there about 6:25 p.m.

When he went in the side door, he was in the kitchen. They were just finishing dinner. Carroll was there as well as one of his sons and his wife. Paul briefly highlighted why he was there. He told them how RA's name had come up in the trial, that Nance and Tisdale had implicated him as the cooker when the meth lab caught fire, and that he was just trying to find out information about RA and maybe talk to him.

Carroll Trail immediately told him that R. A. Boone was a really good guy and that he, like his dad, was a law-abiding citizen. He also had something to say about Sam Nance. Trail said he had been one of the officers who once arrested Sam for cooking meth in a metal building in Pemiscot County Missouri, but that he had retired before the case was settled. He added that he didn't think Nance had ever been convicted of a crime.

Paul began to relate the testimony about R. A. Boone and all the inconsistencies in Nance and Tisdale's testimony at trial. Carroll pretty much ended the conversation by saying, "I ain't talking about Sam Nance. His dad, Sonny Nance, is one of my good friends. I ain't got nothin' to say about the Nances."

Paul drove away from the house knowing he had learned at least one thing from his trip: Southeast Missouri was certainly Nance's area. Not only did he have an *in* with the authorities in Pemiscot County, but he knew the sheriff of New Madrid County where Portageville was located was Sonny Nance's *best friend*. No wonder Sam Nance and Timmy Tisdale had both escaped punishment for crimes we would later learn they had committed. The fix there was truly in!

Chapter 5

Keith Hawkins and Christmas and New Year's Eves

Paul visited me at Mason on Christmas Day. He said we had always been together on that day and it would continue to be that way. The day before, on the twenty-fourth, Paul and Jen had gone to visit Kara at the Hardeman County jail, where she was being held.

The family celebrated Christmas as Paul's house. This was the first Christmas we had not celebrated as a family at Mom and Dad's in Rector, Arkansas. My son, Carey, showed up but got mad at everyone laughing and enjoying themselves and left and went off to be by himself. As soon as they celebrated Christmas that morning, Paul came to Mason to see me.

Keith had ended up with fifty pounds of Christmas boxes too. Between us, we actually had about ninety pounds of Christmas goodies. I had two laundry bags on the side of my locker as full of goods as they could be. Considering the commissary the men owed me from the cigarettes, I wouldn't have to go to commissary for months. We also got a rather large Christmas bag of goods from the prison.

During November and December, Keith had filed at least fifty or more cop-outs (requests to staff) to medical to be taken out to the hospital in order to have the wires removed from his teeth and jaws because of injuries received in a fight. The wires were wired around each tooth, top and bottom, and connected by vertical wires. I even submitted a dozen or more requests myself to medical on his behalf. They never responded.

On Christmas Eve, after the ten o'clock count, we were locked in our cell. I was lying on the bottom bunk, and Keith was on the upper bunk. All at once, he hopped down out of the bunk and said, "I am going to take these wires off my teeth and out of my mouth."

I said, "How are you going to do that?"

He replied, "Just watch!"

He took off his institutional shirt and T-shirt and was bare-chested. He dug around in his locker and came up with a pair of nail clippers and a small pair of cuticle scissors. He stood in front of the metal sink, looked into the metal mirror, and began clipping and winding the wire around and around off each tooth. Every time he clipped or snipped, I got anxious about the whole process.

I watched as he unwound the wire off the first two teeth on the bottom left of his mouth. He had blood and slobber running down his chin from both sides of his mouth and onto his chest. His eyes were watering, and every now and then he would hit the wall with his fist. It took him three hours to get all the wires unwound off his bottom teeth. He gargled saltwater and did what he could to stop the bleeding. The pain must have been excruciating. The wire was a continuous strip that must have been five inches long when unwound. I had spent much of the three hours curled up in my bunk facing the wall and not watching. I had the pillow wrapped around my head to cover my ears from the incessant sound of metal on metal each time he snipped or clipped. It was a hard way to spend Christmas Eve. It was even harder for Keith.

He repeated the same process on the upper teeth a week later on New Year's Eve. It was extremely cruel for them to make that man suffer so much. It was bad enough they didn't have the wires removed months before as they were supposed to do, but they had waited until one of the vertical wires had broken and let his mouth get all twisted up on the outside. Additionally, they had never taken him back to get his badly broken nose checked. It was obviously not set properly and resulted in loud snoring and difficulty for Keith. He had suffered tremendously. Removing the wires should have been done by a professional, but it was not. He never saw a doctor or anyone from medical while he was at the facility. He was treated inhumanely once he returned to CCA Mason after his original trip to the hospital months before and then his time at 201 Poplar Medical Isolation Wing back in the fall.

Chapter 6

Incidentals

The new year begun pretty much the same as the old one had ended. Men were continuously coming and going to and from the institution. There were some real characters that passed through during those months.

A young white man was there waiting to go to trial for arson. He was guilty. He was caught at the fire. He had burned down his father-in-law's business. He had the same public defender as Kara, June Riley. She must have made five or six trips to Mason to visit her client for his case. For their meetings, they used the same small office I had been in with the presentence report lady. The door to the room had a four-inch window about twelve inches long to see into the room. It was almost right across from our dorm (B-Pod). Each time he was called for a lawyer visit, men begun coming up with excuses to leave the dorm and go see the counsel, or go to medical or laundry, or anywhere else just so they could go down the hallway while he was visiting June Riley, his attorney. Everyone else in the dorm would just crowd around the door in the unit to get as close as possible to the office across the hallway.

The reason for the great interest in his lawyer visit was that this inmate always walked in and exposed himself to June. He actually just whipped it out and laid it on the desk right in front of where she sat. Guys in the hallway witnessed it by walking by at just the right time and looking in the window and seeing it happen. The rest just listened from across the hallway for her scream and his hysterical laughter. Needless to say, his visits with June Riley never lasted very long. He knew he was going to plead guilty anyway.

There was another interesting man that was in our unit at that time. He lived upstairs in room 210. It was located at the farthest end of the range. It was as far away from the door and the shower stalls on the wall in the dayroom as possible. He had a daily ritual. He was about 45 years old, black, and about 6 feet, and 350 pounds. At every evening meal, he went around asking each man for any food he didn't eat. I saw him pile food a foot and a half high on his tray. He would take it to his room and eat every single bite.

After chow, he stripped down naked and came down the far stairs and across the dayroom and headed to the shower stalls on the wall near the front door. All he brought with him was a bar of soap. He would turn the water on, walk under the water until he was soaking wet, turn the water off, step out from under the nozzle, and step back. He would take the soap then and lather up his entire body until he was just covered in soap and walk back across the dayroom, up the stairs, into his room, and close the automatically locking door. He would then be in his cell for the night. He did this night after night, week after week, for several months.

The third strange character during those months was a very lightskinned black man with freckles who showed up in our unit about 8:30 p.m. on a Sunday night. He was slightly tongue-tied, and he told us everyone called him Red. It fit him perfectly. He actually had a red tint to his skin, and his freckles even looked dark red. This man had the warmest smile on his face I have ever seen. He was a very, very gentle older man who claimed he had no idea why he was there and that he had not been arrested or accused of a crime as far as he knew. He said a man just showed up at his house and asked him if he wanted to take a ride. He said the man drove him here and let him out and then just drove away. We thought, "Yeah, I'll bet that's just what happened!" Arriving there on a Sunday was also unusual.

The first count they did that night after he had arrived stumped us all. The officers kept messing up count. It was him. They had no idea who he was or why he was there. They had no paperwork on him. He had a prison uniform on but nothing else, and the laundry guy wasn't even working. They had to get him some bedclothes, some additional clothing, underwear, socks, washcloths, and towels.

They had the same problem with counts on Monday, and they kept coming up one tray short at meals. He was "off the books" as they say. Same thing on Tuesday.

We had church on Tuesday night, and a volunteer from the outside came in to conduct the service. We asked Red if he would like to go with us. He smiled from ear to ear and said, "Boy, would I!" At 7:00 p.m., we went and got him. He lived in 209 right next to the lathered-up man.

One of the traditions of the church at Mason was to always recognize new men in the service. He raised his hand when they asked about new men and told the group his name was Red. He told everyone how much he loved the Lord, smiling the entire time. After a few praise songs, Remy asked if anyone had a testimony or a song they would like to sing. Red raised his hand. He walked up front still smiling and said he wanted to sing. He sang a song many of us had learned as children at church called "Jesus Loves Me." He was slightly tongue-tied and sang rather quietly, but it was almost angelic. It was the most beautiful, genuine, heartfelt song I had ever heard. When he finished and shuffled back to his seat with that big smile on his face, the room remained absolutely still and quiet. Time had stopped. There was not one man in the room, except Red, that wasn't weeping. We sat that way several minutes. No one wanted to break the spell. The song was a service in itself and so much more. Every heart in the room had been deeply touched. Mine included.

The next morning at 6:00 a.m. when our cell doors were all unlocked, we noticed Red was missing. None of the officers working our unit could tell us who he was, why he was there, or where he went. Ms. Cain said she had checked herself, and there simply was no paperwork on that man in 209.

If I have ever seen an angel, I am convinced it was Red. He didn't look like my idea of an angel or Hollywood's idea of an angel either. But if you had heard him sing "Jesus Loves Me," well, you'd know that Jesus really did love him. What joy Red had brought into that place for forty-eight hours!

Chapter 7

January 11, 1999

I was adjusting to incarceration. However, at bedtime, the loneliness, desperation, and anxiety would come in a rush. At those times, I would just pray and shake and tremble at the enormity of it all.

Throughout December and January, I had continued calling home at 6:00 p.m. just as Kara had. Our talking and hearing each other's voice was an anchor that helped keep us stable. They made each day easier. Thank God for Cockroach, the inmate in my pod that made sure I had a telephone at 6:00 p.m. seven nights a week.

On Tuesday night, just after chow and my call to Kara, I was in my cell writing Kara a letter. It was January 10, 1999. Keith was in his bed sitting up working a timeline on his case. He was scheduled to be sentenced in February, and he wasn't going down without a fight. There was a quiet knock at our door. I looked up to see Officer (Mrs.) Cain and Officer (Ms.) McDaniel coming through our door. That was not unusual. They stopped by the room often.

I immediately said, "Hey, come on in, ladies. What can I do for you beautiful correction officer ladies?" When neither one smiled, I knew something was up. I got up and said, "What's wrong?"

Ms. Cain said, "Jack, they told me to come tell you to pack up. You're leaving."

I said, "You're kidding!"

"No," she said, "you are supposed to get ready. They will be coming to get you sometime before daylight."

I realized she was serious. I said, "Where am I going, Ms. Cain?"

She said, "I don't know for sure. I do know you will be put in a van and taken to the Memphis Airport. You might be going to Oklahoma City to be processed into the Bureau of Prisons."

I was stunned. I had known this day was coming. Now that it was here, I didn't want to leave. I was afraid. I had become comfortable in Mason. I was only thirty-five miles out of Memphis. I knew how everything worked here. I had friends. I had Keith. Most of all, I had the phone calls to Kara. How would she feel if our phone calls were over? My god! When would I hear her voice again?

I looked at Ms. Cain and said, "Thank you, Ms. Cain. I am glad it was you who told me." She came across the room, and I noticed the tears in her eyes. She hugged me real good, as did Ms. McDaniel. They both told me they would certainly miss me. I appreciated all they had done to make my time better. We had become friends. They wished me luck and hurried out of the cell. I knew they would both be off and gone by the time I left, and I would never see them again.

Keith had remained silent the whole time. Now he jumped off the bed and hugged me and said, "Damn, Jack, I am sure going to miss you!"

I said, "Not as much as I'll miss you. It just dawned on me that I have not been in prison when you weren't there. Even when you were out on medical, I knew you were coming back. It will be harder on me without you, Keith. I really do love you, brother!"

He said, "Me too."

I told him, "Well, don't just stand there. Let's start going through all this stuff. I can't take it with me." I had accumulated a great deal in the five months I had been there, not to mention all the Christmas items.

I had those two bags of Christmas goodies, and I thought of all the commissary those guys owed me for the cigarettes. I would never collect that. Boy, did they get a good deal! I told Keith to pick through it all and keep what he wanted and I would give the rest to Nacho. He said, "Just give all that stuff to Nacho. I don't know where I would put it. I have fifty pounds of stuff myself. Just give it to Nacho." I told him he would have to do that because I would be gone before I could see Nacho.

I thought about the two-piece Bible I had picked up and read when I first arrived. I thought about the great Bible studies and our prayer group and our church. I had a lot I would miss besides the men that had become such close friends. When a person goes through something horrendous with someone, he instantly forms deep bonds, like soldiers entrenched in war. I had formed those kinds of bonds.

They came to get me at 2:00 a.m. I stayed in the holding cells off the small office until around 4:00 a.m. They dressed me out in plain khaki pants with an elastic waistband and a white T-shirt and flat blue slip-on tennis shoes. They had me place all my things I wanted to keep in boxes to be shipped to my brother's house. It was the morning of January 11, 1999, and I was leaving Mason. I realized they didn't give me a coat.

Chapter 8

The Federal Bureau of Prisons

January 11 was Paul's birthday. It was also Don Hornsby's birthday. He was my best friend back in Rector, Arkansas. I always thought it very odd that Paul and Don would share the same birth date. January 11 would also be my first day in federal prison.

We left Mason that morning just before 8:00 a.m. There were seven of us placed in the van. I had ridden in that van or one like it many times going to and from court in Memphis. I was handcuffed and shackled with the black box as were the other men in the van. This ride would be different. We were not going to the Clifford Davis Building in Memphis, nor would we return to Mason. We ended up at Wilson Airfield, an auxiliary airstrip near Memphis International Airport.

The men in the van said we most likely were going to Oklahoma City or Atlanta to a designation center. From there, we would be processed into the system and then placed in whatever facility they assigned us. I still had hopes in Millington, as my judge had suggested, but the men at Mason had convinced me that with the length of my sentence, I wasn't going to Millington.

We arrived near 9:00 a.m. While we waited on the ConAir transport to arrive, several buses and other vans arrived. Soon there were maybe ten or fifteen. Federal officers were everywhere wearing flak jackets and carrying either shotguns or military assault rifles. They all dressed in black and had "US Marshal" stenciled on the back of whatever they were wearing. They looked like a SWAT team.

We were told the plane was supposed to arrive at 9:10 a.m. It didn't get there until closer to 10:00 a.m. When it taxied to a stop, stairs were placed up against the plane to a previously unnoticed door. The prisoner movement began. It was beautifully choreographed. All prisoners disembarked their van or bus and stood in line next to that vehicle. Some of the inmates, like me, had on just a T-shirt. It was very cold and damp that January morning.

The armed Marshals spread out all around the plane and all over the tarmac. They were attentive and watchful and somewhat menacing. The first action involved prisoners on the plane. About forty inmates, male and female, were ushered off the plane. The stairs were really steep, and the inmates had a difficult time negotiating the stairs while shackled. I watched as several stumbled on the stairs. When they had all disembarked, they were placed in a line of their own.

The second phase began with prisoners being loaded on the plane. Each of the waiting lines took their turn. Eventually, they got to our line by the van. One of the female US Marshals had a clipboard and called out names. As a prisoner's name was called, he marched to the plane and became climbing the stairs. Climbing up was even more difficult that climbing down.

When there were only two of us left, the Marshal called our names and pointed to the van to our right and said, "You two, get in the Memphis van." I didn't know what the Memphis van meant, but I did want to get out of the cold, so I did as she told me as quickly as possible. As we approached the van, an officer stepped off and checked our names on his clipboard. He then removed our handcuffs and shackles and replaced them with a different set. This set did not include the black box. The officer from Mason took their shackles with them.

We were placed in the Memphis van along with five or six other inmates that had disembarked from the plane. They knew where we were going. They said we were going to FCI Memphis. It was a medium-high-security facility. Apparently, I would not be going to the camp at Millington. As it turned out, the other man from Mason that had ridden with me from Mason did go to Millington.

On January 20, 1999, just nine days after I was transported, some officers came into Kara's cell at the Hardeman County jail with boxes and told her to pack up as she was leaving. Kara had no idea where she was going either. She had talked to Paul on the phone and knew I had been transferred and was at FCI Memphis.

On January 21, 1999, she was placed in a van and taken to the airstrip where I had been taken. When the ConAir transport plane arrived, Kara was flown to Oklahoma City, Oklahoma, for processing. She spent a week there before being taken by bus to the FCI Low facility at Carswell Air Force Base in Fort Worth, Texas.

Kara and I were both now in the system and in the custody of the Federal Bureau of Prisons. We were both behind double-chain-link fences with razor wire on top. It was scary and gut-wrenching to leave the familiar places we had been for the last five months and end up where we were. I hoped we could handle it.

I was also wondering when I might get to talk to Kara again. To just hear her voice and to hear her laugh, or even to hear her cry. I knew he would be wondering the same thing. We didn't even know if we could write each other. We wouldn't be able to speak to one another again for four years.

Chapter 9

The Federal Correctional Institution at Memphis

Two US Marshals escorted me to the front gate of FCI Memphis on January 11, 1999, where two correction officers were waiting for me inside the gate. My shackles were removed and given to the US Marshals. I was then handcuffed and shackled by the correction officers with shackles that belonged to the facility.

I was taken to receiving and discharge (R and D) and placed in a holding cell and remained there for several hours. No one seemed in a hurry to get to me. Eventually, they brought me lunch inside the receiving cell. It was difficult to eat while handcuffed. Later, I was removed from the holding cell and taken into a changing area. My shackles were removed, and I was told to undress completely.

There was a check for identifying tattoos (I had none) and a full body search, which meant first I opened my mouth as wide as I could and stretched the jaws on each side with my index fingers to let the officer see into my mouth. He then told me to slowly run my fingers through my hair. My hair wasn't long, so that was easy. He then told me to turn around, bend over, and spread both my butt cheeks apart and to squat and cough. It was extremely humiliating to have another man look at your anus. I was given prison khakis and told to put clothes in a container nearby. He then handcuffed me and put me back in the holding cell. Each of the other eight inmates in the holding cell went through the same.

I found myself sitting next to a seventy-nine-year-old white man named Jerry. He was in poor health and used cane to get around. I couldn't help but wonder what crime he could have committed at his age and physical condition. Jerry told me he had been farming four hundred acres of farmland planter with marijuana. He said he had it baled and stored in a barn like hay. Jerry said he had over four hundred bales in the barn and more growing in the field. He had received a life sentence. Jerry's wife was also incarcerated. She ended up in a women's facility in Bryan, Texas. She was serving a twenty-year sentence. At one time, he had been a Pentecostal preacher.

The correction officers began taking us out of the cells one at a time. Although handcuffed, we were no longer shackled in the R and D area. We went one at a time to interview with a psychologist. Our interview exchange went something like this:

Psychologist: Mr. Phillips, you have an extremely long sentence. Would you like me to set up an appointment schedule for you now?

Jack: For what?

Psychologist: For the depression and mental struggles you are going to go through.

Jack: I am not going to be depressed and have mental troubles. I'm a Christian, I have faith. Even if I did have trouble, I would talk to a chaplain, not a psychologist.

Psychologist: Well, we'll see about that, won't we?

Jack: I guess we will.

I knew I would not seek the advice of a secular humanist. I did not believe or have any confidence in their mumbo jumbo. I had been a Christian for too long and had no confidence in the psychobabble theories.

Eventually, we were all lined up and marched to laundry. There was an officer in charge of laundry in the room and three inmates working in there. We were taken into the laundry room itself and put through the process of trying on pants and shirts. Eventually we were given our *prison* clothes (all khaki). We got three of everything. The T-shirts, boxers, and socks were all old and faded yellow or at least what one would call off-white. The clothes were terrible and ill-fitting. The socks I received were so old they had no elastic at all to hold them up. The officer there was extremely rude. Questioning him about the clothes or exchanging what you had been given was not allowed. We dressed in a white jumpsuit and put our clothes into a laundry bag. The last thing we received was a bedroll with sheets, blankets, and a pillow. There were also small hygiene items like a small tube of toothpaste, a cheap toothbrush, and a clear liquid in a small bottle that was supposed to be soap and shampoo.

The officer said we would be going to Memphis A-Unit, where we would be in a holding area for new prisoners for a few days until we completed A and O, which meant Admission and Orientation. The escorting officer paired us up and said the man we were paired with would be our cellmate. I was paired with Jerry, the old man and marijuana farmer. I knew even with his cane Jerry would have a hard time walking across the compound to the unit the officer said was Memphis-A. Grabbing his radio, the officer ordered the compound closed. That meant that all the inmates on the compound at that moment had to go inside. There could be no inmates on the yard as handcuffed men were being moved. Because we were handcuffed, we were easy targets for stabbing if someone had a grudge against any one of us. He told us to get in single file and follow him. Jerry was struggling with his laundry bag and bedroll and his cane. I took his laundry bag and carried it for him along with all my stuff.

We had to make a detour back to R and D for some paperwork. As soon as we entered R and D, I saw a white officer, twenty to twenty-five years old. As we got near, he kind of walked toward us with his eyes focused on me. I assumed I had done something wrong. As he got near, he said, "Coach Phillips! Aren't you Coach Phillips that used to work at Carlisle High School?"

I said "Yes, that's me."

He began walking along beside us as we crossed the compound and said, "I'm David DePriest. I used to play football at Martin High School."

I said, "Yeah, DePriest, I remember you. You wore number eleven."

He smiled and said, "That's right. I played baseball and ran track too."

I told him, "You were a really good athlete. I remember you."

In football, we beat his team 49–0 his senior year. It was 42–0 at halftime, and we subbed and quit trying to score. He was a good player on a bad team. He ran the ball, played defense, ran back punts and kickoffs, and never came off the field for a rest. He was tough as nails.

I told him, "You were really a good football player. We focused all our attention on stopping you. I know you really took a beating that night, but you got up every single time. You earned my respect. I'll bet you had trouble getting up out of bed the next morning."

He toughed and said, "Coach, I didn't even get up until three o'clock in the afternoon! I was sore for days."

By then we had reached the Memphis A-Unit. It was a round unit with Unit-A on the right and Unit-B on the left. We had gone by Beale Unit (A and B) and Delta Unit (A and B) and arrived at Memphis Unit (A and B).

Tennessee Unit (A and B) was further down, and Shelby Unit (A and B) was closed, and there was construction work going on in that building. They said it had been destroyed during the riots in 1994, as had Tennessee and some of the other units. Shelby would be the last one to be repaired. It never opened while I was at FCI Memphis. The units were all circular. I had never read in the papers or heard about riots there in 1994.

Jerry and I ended up being the last in line. It was all he could do to make it there, and everyone else had passed us by. I had to let him hang on my arm or he wouldn't have made it. He really needed a wheelchair. Officer DePriest held the door at Memphis Unit-A for us. The dayroom was straight ahead, and cells circled around both right and left from the door. There were cells downstairs and a range of cells upstairs. All of us were placed in cells downstairs and to the right of the door. Because we were last, we ended up in the cell closest to the door, Cell A-101.

We entered the room, and the officer and Officer DePriest both left. Jerry sat down on the bottom bunk, and I sat our laundry bags on the floors in front of the two half lockers. They were about waist-high with double doors on the front. They both had four or five metal shelves inside. I discovered they would hold more than they first appeared.

Jerry just sat on the bed trying to recover from the long walk. I began to reach into my bag to take the things out and put them in my locker. Before I pulled out the first item, an inmate that lived in Memphis Unit-A walked into the cell. He walked over to my locker, reached into his pant pocket, and pulled out three really small plastic bags. He emptied each of the three little bags into three neat piles on my locker. He used his ID card to keep the piles neat. He looked at me and said, "Well, what would you like to have, gentlemen?"

Jerry just sat there, but I said, "Well, what do you have there?"

The inmate pointed at each of the piles and said, "That's marijuana in that pile, cocaine in that pile, and heroin in that pile. What's your pleasure?"

I could hardly believe it. This guy was serious. I hadn't been in my cell sixty seconds, and I was already offered pot, cocaine, and heroin. Honestly, this was prison! Were those drugs that readily available here? What had I gotten myself into?

Jerry and I both told the man we didn't want anything. He just shrugged, scrapped the piles back into the little bags with his ID, stuck them in his pocket and said, "Well, if you change your minds, I'll be in cell no. 129." He left our cell and ducked into cell no. 102 next door to make his sales pitch to them.

I unpacked our bags and put all our stuff in both our lockers. I then helped Jerry up and made his bed and then made mine. It was almost time for 4:00 p.m. count and then chow. We were to wear the white jump suit until we completed A and O. At chow, everyone stared at the new men. Later we had 10:00 p.m. count and were locked in our room for the night.

Three TVs had been on in the dayroom the entire time. However, we couldn't hear them. At Mason, we had one TV that was turned up on full volume all the time. Here, you had to have a Walkman radio to pick up the frequencies on the FM for the televisions. The counselor in Memphis Unit-A had come by and given each of us a radio to use until we left the unit. The radio was checked out to us, and there were all kinds of threats if it wasn't returned along with the headphones that came with the radios. We could also pick up AM and FM radio stations on the radios. That really helped relieve the monotony.

Over the course of the next week, we attended A and O meetings. All the functions of the institution were explained. We were all given a small handbook with the rules and punishments for violating said rules. We learned about the following:

- Count times
- Ten-minute moves
- Visitation days and hours
- Mail and the mailroom
- Phones
- That we had to get a job
- The dress code
- Unit cleanliness
- Various services from medical to psychological
- The Chapel Services Department
- Rec yard times and rules and regulations
- Chow hall demeanor and function

It was a lot to absorb. It would take all of us weeks to fully understand those procedures and adapt to them. I found at least three men I had known at Mason. I sure was glad to see them because there were some really hard people there. Some were doing multiple life sentences. Quite a few had already been incarcerated for thirty or more years. These living conditions were all foreign to me. I was eventually assigned to Beale Unit-B. I was placed in cell no. 313. It was downstairs and right next to the only downstairs shower. Here is where I would spend the next fourteen months of life.

Chapter 10

Tank and Guy

My cellmate in Beale-B, no. 313, was a man from Montana. His name was Guy Rose. He was an Aryan Nation guy complete with lightning bolts and swastikas tattooed on his neck. He was a white supremacist wannabe. He was about five feet ten inches and three hundred pounds with a large gap between his front two teeth and a buzz cut on top.

Paul had sent me money, and it had been added to my account. I now had an ID and a BOP number that would identify me throughout the whole system. It was an eight-digit number. My last three numbers were 076, which indicated I had caught my case in West Tennessee. Numbers 075 and 074 indicated Middle Tennessee and East Tennessee. Everyone's last three numbers identified where he caught his case. The military had their numbers, and illegal immigrants had their identifying numbers in the BOP too. It was an ingenious and necessary system.

I had submitted my phone number requests and visitation form requests and had my first team meeting with my counselor, case manager, and unit manager. I found out I would be scheduled for team meetings every six months to check my progress in the institution. It was at this first team meeting that I saw my protected release date with good time credit would be August 17, 2017. Without good time credit, it would be November 2019. Considering it was only January 1999, those dates seemed impossible to comprehend. I had a long, long way to go, and the good time credit was important. An inmate received good time credit for good behavior and for progressing in the system. Regardless of how much one earned, he was still going to do a minimum of 85 percent of his sentence. That figure actually turned out to be 87–1/2 percent because of some insane way the BOP figured good time credit.

I quickly learned that many men at this facility had longer sentences than I did. One man who lived right upstairs above me in Beale-B, no. 413, had five life sentences. Two men I knew from Mason had thirty and forty years respectively. I ran across some men from Northeast Arkansas, one of these men I had actually met in 1971. He didn't remember me, but I remembered him. He had been busted for meth in 1987, the first year of the mandatory sentences. Even though it was his first ever criminal offense, he and three of his codefendants were doing at least thirty-five-year sentences. They had already completed almost twelve years. My sentence was really long, but it was certainly not unique at a medium-high facility. I also learned an inmate never mentioned if his sentence was about to run out and he was about to be released. Inmates that were going to be there for decades or for life simply did not want to hear about someone getting out.

I was really happy to see Tank at FCI Memphis. He and I had become good friends at Mason. I was only with him for about two months before he left and came to FCI Memphis, but we had become close. He was a relatively young, articulate black man. He was physically built and muscled up. I had actually coached football against him and his learn. He had attended a really good private Christian school. His parents were both college educated and intelligent. Paul had become good friends with them (especially his mom) through visitations at Mason. Tank had been taking a psychology class to finish up a degree from Memphis State University. My brother had actually purchased a textbook for him, and his mom had given my brother his money back. Tank was well informed, and we had many meaningful and intelligent discussions. He was well-read on a variety of topics. Good, meaningful conversations like that were always hard to find in prison.

The first day I was in Beale-B, the same unit where Tank lived, I decided to go to commissary. Some gave me a commissary list, and

I carefully marked what I needed: some sweats, tennis shoes, a radio, a pen and paper, and envelopes and stamps to write letters. When I finished my list, it totaled $123. There were a few soft drinks added in there too.

Tank walked up to the door and knocked. I said, "Come on in, Tank."

He said, "Coach, are you going to the store?"

I said, "Yes, I am going right after four-o'clock count."

He asked me if I wanted him to go with me, but I told him no, I wasn't getting that much and I could carry it myself.

Tank just smiled at me and said, "No, Coach, do you *need* me to go with you?"

Again, I said, "No thanks. I appreciate it, but I'm not buying that much."

Tank said, "Coach, that's not what I am talking about. What are you going to do if a man or a group of men decide they want to take all your commissary? That's why I'm asking you if you need me to go with you."

That had never crossed my mind. What would I do if that happened? Truthfully, probably not much. I looked at Tank and said, "Tank, they might take my commissary. That is certainly a possibility. But they had better be willing to kill me because I will fight back. Look, I've got twenty years to do in here. I have to stand on my own. You won't be around while I do all this time. I might as well stand up today."

He nodded his head and said, "Okay, Coach. You take care of it then." He turned and walked away from the door.

The man that lived next door came from the store with a laundry bag of items, and I asked him if it was crowded up there. He said, "No, there were only three men there when I left."

I decided I would go and hope I made it back before count. It was only about 3:00 p.m. If I was lucky, I would get in and out before count. I grabbed my bag and list and headed toward the store. I didn't make it. I would have to go back to the store after four o'clock.

As soon as count was over, I hustled to the store. I was the second man in line. I shopped and got my commissary and headed back toward the unit. It was only about 4:40 p.m., but it was already getting dark. I saw a few men headed to and from the store and others moving around going other places. I wasn't fifty yards from my unit. As I walked, I couldn't help but look around recalling what Tank had warned me about. I half-expected a group of men to come try to take my commissary. I kept turning my head looking from side to side. I made it back to the unit and breathed a sigh of relief.

Guy was in the cell when I got back. We had nothing in common. He was in his early thirties but had already done about six years in state on some charge. He was institutionalized. We couldn't even find much to talk about because he was a nut. He was an Aryan Nation member, a product of the prison system. His best friend in the unit was Harold Blue—or, as he was called, Monique. Monique had started at a USP and worked down to the medium low. He/she was notorious for his/her Saturday-night walk-bys. Each Saturday night, he/she got drunk, put on a short tie-dyed T-shirt and sandals, and strolled the unit. He/she went door to door in the unit offering blow jobs for a book of stamps. Anything else you might want to do was also possible if an inmate had the stamps. This was a fifty-something skinny black male dressing and acting as a female. It was disgusting. This was Guy's best friend. Postage stamps were the currency in prison. I thought it was cigarettes. I was wrong.

Besides just being a sicko, there was something scary in Harold Blue's eyes. I don't know if they were just missing something or if they had seen too much. Monique was just as scary looking. I really didn't want the he/she hanging around our room, and I told Guy that.

It wasn't long after I put my store purchases away and locked my locker with my new combination lock that chow was called. Guy didn't go with me; he was in the dayroom talking to Monique, but he hustled up to food service passing me along the way and sat right across the aisle from me after we both got our tray. He sat down as I did and was still there after I left.

I returned to the cell and walked in and saw things weren't right in the cell. My locker was standing wide open, and there was no sign of my combination lock. I walked to the locker and opened both doors and looked in and saw that everything was gone but the institutional toiletry items I had been given when I first arrived. All $123 worth of commissary I had just purchased was gone. My lock had even been stolen.

I immediately thought of Guy and Monique. Monique didn't show up for chow, and Guy seemed to be establishing an alibi by sitting right across from me. I felt in my bones that those two were responsible. Not many people even saw or knew I had gone to commissary. I also had an instinct of what was required when these things happened in prison. An inmate didn't go to the authorities (except I had to go to my counselor to get permission to buy another radio). If I discovered who took my things, it was expected of me to retaliate with lethal force. I would be expected to respond in the most violent way I could. Killing them would not be considered too severe. If I discovered who took my things and did nothing, everything I ever bought or had would be taken. Weakness would be exploited all the time and to the fullest extreme. I couldn't be weak. An inmate had to do what that culture demanded he do or suffer the consequences.

Guy stayed gone most of the night. Later, when I was alone, Tank appeared on my door. He had a serious look on his face. I was about to get an education on prison life and about who Tank really was. He said, "Coach, I heard somebody stole all the store you bought?"

I said, "Yeah, Tank. They even took my combination lock."

He said, "Do you know who did it, Coach? If you do, just tell me. If I find out who did it, I'll kill the son of a bitch myself. I swear to God, he won't see the sun come up tomorrow."

I told Tank I had my suspicious about who did it, but I really couldn't prove it. I told him, "Besides, it's only $123. That's not worth killing someone over."

Tank said, "It's not about the amount, Coach. Just tell me who you *think* did it, and I'll cut their damn throat! This is prison. Jack, I am an *enforcer* in this unit for the gang that runs this yard. It's an insult to me for them to steal from you. Besides, you are my friend. I'll promise you this, no one will ever steal from you again. Who do you think did it, Coach?"

I had never heard Tank curse in the months I had known him and in all the conversations we had. I told him, "I am not going to say. If I find out for sure who did it, I'll let you know. And, Tank, thanks for caring."

He told me he was going to spread the word that everyone had better keep their hands off me and my property. I couldn't believe the cold look I had seen in Tank's eyes. He had changed right in front of me. He was not making idle threats. He had meant every single word he had said. I had never seen that side of him. I couldn't imagine him as a gangbanger, but there he stood. I was glad he was my friend.

Shortly after that, Guy returned to the room. He climbed in the bottom bunk, and I got up in my bunk on the top. I said, "Guy, are you asleep?"

He said, "No, I'm just laying here."

I told him, "You know, somebody stole all the stuff I bought at the store. They even took my lock. All I have left are the few toiletry items they gave me and the few things that were left in this locker from the last man."

He said, "I heard you got ripped off."

I jumped down off the top bunk and stood over him and looked him right into the eyes. I said, "Yeah, but I've got a big surprise for the thieves. First, I am pretty sure who pulled this off. I have a real surprise in store."

He sat up on the bunk and said, "You know who took your stuff? Who was it?"

I wanted to scream "You and Monique!" but I didn't. Instead, I said, "Do you know what I am in here for?"

He said, "No, I don't."

I told him, "I am in here because I am a chemist. I had a drug lab, and they busted me." I started pouring some shampoo and soap and whatever else was in my locker in the lid of one of the bottles and stirring it with a pencil. I told him, "I am mixing up a little acid. All I have to do is add some of this NACL [salt], and this little concoction will become a powerful acid."

He said, "What are you going to do with that?"

I told him, "I am going to wait until those thieves are sleeping, and then I am going to dip this pencil in that acid and just drip a small drop on each eyelid while they sleep. That acid will eat their eyes right out of their head. Once I blind them, I am going to abuse them and do every unnatural thing I can think of to their bodies." I leaned over to him and looked him in the eyes and said, "And then I am going to use this acid to remove key parts of their body!"

He sat there wide-eyed looking at me and said, "You better not keep that acid in here, Jack. You'll get us both in, trouble."

I said, "This!" I stuck my little finger tip into the solution and touched it to my tongue. I told him, "This is nothing until I add the salt. There's nothing here to get in trouble about. I'm not adding the salt until I am sure they are asleep and I'm ready to use it."

At six o'clock the next morning, when they unlocked our door, Guy went to the lieutenant's office and checked himself into protective custody and was admitted to Segregated Housing (the Shu). He only came out once in the next fourteen months and made it about thirty feet from the Shu (Segregate Housing Unit) when he saw me coming, turned around, and checked back in. I never saw him again after that brief encounter. I didn't kill him, but I certainly got rid of him in my own way.

Chapter 11

Morgan Green

M organ Green became one of my best friends at FCI Memphis. He was by far the most interesting character I had met behind bars. He was sixty-nine years old and smoked Camels with no filters. He had been incarcerated since 1948 and had not been free from prison for a full calendar year since then. Imagine, fifty-one years locked up. He had been incarcerated on a bank robbery charge with the feds since 1972. His rap sheet (history of criminal activity) was page after page. He had not had a visitor since 1972 and had no idea what the visiting room at FCI Memphis looked like. His record was supposedly the longest of anyone from the state of Alabama. He had kidnapped an Alabama prison official at knifepoint in one escape and had a series of escapes in his history. He had served decades in maximum security prisons in the state of Alabama.

He lived in my unit, but I actually became acquainted with him because of softball. The softball field at FCI Memphis was not on the rec yard. It sat right in the middle of the compound. Actually, right outside the Beale Unit where we lived. It was warm outside one day, and the softball season was about to begin. He was the official score-keeper for the league. He showed up at my door one day with a ball and two gloves. He said in his gravelly voice, "Boy, can you catch?"

I said, "Yeah, I can catch."

He said, "Can you catch good?"

I told him, "Yes, I can catch. Look, I played college baseball. I can catch."

He told me, "I am a fastball league softball pitcher. I used to be pretty good." Morgan was about 6 feet 4 inches and 195 pounds. He had long arms and had no fat on him and got around good for his age.

We walked out the door and straight to the softball field. He stepped off the distance to the pitcher's mound. I got behind home plate and squatted down. He didn't throw over thirty pitches, but gosh, could he bring it! He could throw a curve, a slider and riser, and a strike with all the pitches.

I found out from him later that when he was younger, he had played on a prison softball team that traveled around and played in large softball tournaments at other prison and military bases. He rattled off at least ten former major league players he had played softball against. I recognized most of them. Some of those major leaguers had been all stars. He told me about pitching no-hitters and perfect games and an incredible streak of scoreless innings in one stretch. He said that he had won numerous MVP awards and had an entire room at his mom's house back then full of trophies for pitching softball. Because of his love of sports and my love of sports, naturally we bonded.

Morgan didn't have an official prison job. He had to hustle. He did laundry for inmates who paid him stamps for the work. Stamps were the currency in prison. I had always thought it was cigarettes. No, it was stamps. You could buy anything with stamps. He said he was one of thirteen children, but all his brothers and sisters and mom and dad had died. He was the only surviving child. He said he knew he had one female cousin that was married and lived in Kentucky, but he didn't know her married name. He had absolutely no financial support from the outside. Many times, he just gave an inmate a commissary list of items to pay for doing that inmate's laundry. I bought him a carton of Camels each month for doing my laundry, and I bought him other items off commissary and just gave them to him because he needed it. He didn't go without. I have never met anyone to this day that knew more about surviving in the prison system. Morgan knew every in and out. He seemed to take me under his wing from the very beginning.

For example, after my commissary was stolen, he volunteered to take his afternoon naps from 1:00–3:00 p.m. in my room on my bunk to keep an eye on things. He was in the unit all day, so he promised me he would go by my room every thirty minutes or so just to check on it. He rarely left the unit except for meals and softball games. I never had anything else stolen out of my room. Between him and Tank, I felt like my possessions were safe.

Tank had explained to me that he was a gangster disciple. He was a lieutenant and an enforcer. He was really bad to the bone. His education, background, and outward aura completely defied his affiliation with a street gang. He once informed me he had talked to the man (the gang leader that ran the prison yard) and that I would always be protected on that compound. He said, "Coach, you are as safe here as any inmate could be. The word is out to everyone. You are off limits." He went on and added, "You have absolutely nothing to fear as long as you are here."

Paul had told me to have Morgan submit a visitation form to add Jen to his visitation list. Since he had no list, she would be the only one on his list. He filled out the form, I sent it to Jen, and she returned it to the institution. She was now on Morgan's visitation list. When Paul and Jen came to visit, Paul asked to visit me, and Jen asked to visit Morgan. He had been there twenty-nine years and had never seen the visitation room. It was encouraging to have him visit with us every Saturday morning.

Chapter 12

Steve Branham, Kara, and Keith

Steve Branham (Red), the inmate we had picked up in the van on a return trip to Mason at the Shelby County Penal Farm, showed up at FCI Memphis only three days after I did. By the time he had finished A and O, Guy had checked into protective custody, and I had no cellmate. Steve was assigned to Beale-B, and we requested he be assigned as my cellmate. I had moved down to the bottom bunk after Guy left, so Steve took the top bunk. I had a good cellie. We got along well. He was college educated, played the guitar, lived in Memphis, and was close to my age (forty-seven). That worked out great, and the timing could not have been better.

Kara had transferred to FCI Carswell at Carswell Air Force base and was under a similar security situation as me. Other inmates that had wives, sisters, mothers, or girlfriends incarcerated in the BOP told me that was maybe the best women's facility in the system. There was a male prison nearby and a medical center and a camp for women. Nevertheless, I worried continually about her being in a real prison.

Kara got a job in UNICOR. UNICOR was commonly referred to as the prison industry. Actually, it was a privately owned corporation. All our prison clothes, shoes, mattresses, pillows, bed clothing, and all the furniture in the prison offices and in most government offices were made by UNICOR. They contracted work out to many private companies and the Defense Department and the Copyright and Patent Office. At Memphis, they made these one-thousand-foot-long bundles of wires used on ships and in aircraft for the military.

Each tube of wires carried thousands of colored wires. At Carswell, UNICOR was really a large computer room. They had a contract to do the typing/printing you see under the photographs of cars and trucks in *Auto Trader* magazines and similar publications that sell cars and trucks. When they lost that contract, they began doing copyrights and patents for the United States government. Kara was employee of the month for eleven straight months at one time. She was making more than three hundred dollars a month. She actually sent me money at one point to buy some new tennis shoes. I was glad she had everything she needed.

I guess the biggest surprise came with a phone call from Kara to Paul the same day she arrived at Carswell. The conversation went something like this:

Kara: Paul, I want you to have Phillip Watson check and see if Jack and I can do our time at the same place.

Paul: Kara, I don't think they have coed prisons anymore. (They had actually stopped that in 1972.)

Kara: Well, they have it here. There are men and women, couples, here. I've seen them walking around holding hands and even kissing. The stay in the same cell together. I want that for Jack and me.

Paul: I will check on it then, Kara.

When Paul told me about it on the phone, I told him, "The last facility that did that was Lexington, Kentucky, and they stopped that after 1972."

Paul just said, "That is what I thought."

Bless her heart, the very next night she called Paul again. She told him, "Paul, you know those men I saw here with their wives or girlfriends?"

Paul said, "Yeah."

"Well," Kara explained, "they weren't men. They looked like men. They walked like men. They dressed like men. But they weren't men. So never mind about the coed facilities. You don't have to check with Phillip." Homosexuality in the women's prisons was much more prevalent than in the men's facilities.

Keith Hawkins had also called Paul. He had finally been sentenced. He was given a seventy-month sentence in early February. He had already done about twelve months at Mason, so Keith only had about five years left.

Keith showed up at FCI Memphis just a few days later in early February. I was so happy to see him. While he was processing through A and O, Steve had an opportunity to move into an upstairs end room with a nice white guy from Oklahoma. The advantage to that room was that it was right across from one of the televisions. They could sit in their room and watch television all the time, especially after we were locked in after ten o'clock. They could watch it and hear it all night long. I immediately went to the counselor, Mr. Wren, and asked him to try to get Keith in our unit and moved into my cell as my cellmate. Mr. Wren came through for me and actually pulled it off. Within one month of leaving Keith behind at Mason, we were cellmates again at FCI Memphis. God is good!

Chapter 13

Working at FCI Memphis

After I finished with A and O, I had to find a job. I discovered that FCI Memphis had a GED program and hired inmates as tutors. That sounded perfect to me. I submitted numerous cop-outs (written requests) to work in education. After all, how many certified teachers could they have? I was finally called in for an interview with the supervisor of education. That was a black lady named Strawberry Jackson. It was the least impressive interview I had ever experienced. She told me she would get back with me and let me know about a job.

In the meantime, my name came out on the callout to report to work in AM food service. The name on the callout said I should report to Mr. House in food service. I went over at the one o'clock move and met Mr. House. He was a stocky black man in his late thirties. He assigned me as a cook on the AM shift. I told him I didn't know anything about cooking, but he told me they would teach me everything I needed to know. I asked about my hours, and he said my job would consist of working five days a week from 4:00 a.m. until 12:00 noon or when the noonday meal ended. He said the night officer would come around in the unit and wake me up at 3:00 a.m. to get ready for work. I quickly discovered my job would not involve cooking at all.

When I arrived for work the first day in my kitchen whites (white shirt, white pants, and white socks) as opposed to my khakis, I discovered I was the only white working in the back of the kitchen. There were a few Hispanics, but the rest were black. The dish room, on the other hand, was almost entirely white.

The black cooks treated me with contempt. That is except for one called Captain. He had been a cook in the military for seventeen years and in the BOP for eleven years. He really knew how to cook for large numbers of people, and the food he cooked was always easy to detect. It just tasted better. Whatever he cooked would be the best dish that day at that meal. He treated me respectfully, and we developed a strong friendship.

Basically, my two jobs were to clean out the food grate throughout the shift. It ran from one end of the kitchen to the other right in front of the cooking pots. The large cooking pots had spickets on them at the bottom, which could be opened to empty the water and waste out quickly and easily. It wasn't always just water that came out. Also, the janitors continually swept and pushed trash and water into the grate from anywhere on the floor. The floor was always wet. To clean the grate, I had to raise the grate section by section and remove the solid material from the grate with my hands. I asked about gloves to wear, but Mr. House said, "You don't need no damn gloves, Phillips! Just clean out the damn grate."

I had to get on the floor on my hands and knees to clean out that grate. The cooks all laughed at me. They occasionally threw trash in the trough for me to pick up. It was the nastiest, lousiest job in the kitchen. By the end of my shift, I would be soaked in water.

My second job was to clean out the large pots if the cooks happened to cook baked beans or chili or anything that really stuck to the pot. In that condition, the pot required real scrubbing, not just spraying it down with scalding water. If it was really nasty, they just called for Phillips.

There were so many racial overtones in the kitchen that I couldn't begin to list them all. The black inmates, Mr. House, and all the other black foremen and forewomen seemed to enjoy mistreating Whitey, which was me. Racism?

I also determined from the very beginning not to complain. I had worked since I could walk. I had picked cotton in my grandma's field until I was twelve years old and chopped cotton too. There was no harder work than that. I believed there was dignity in all work regardless of the task. I had been taught a Christian work ethic: "An honest day's work for an honest day's pay." I was also convinced that as a Christian, I should do every job as unto the Lord. As a result, I continually told myself to clean that grate or that pot as if Jesus Christ himself would use it next. That motivated me and gave my work dignity. I worked those horrible jobs at those terrible hours and was paid twelve dollars a month. That only paid for about four phone calls home, which meant I couldn't pay for my phone calls and buy soap or toothpaste or shampoo.

I also served lunch behind the counter in what was called mainline. Mainline meant the entire compound was coming to eat. Captain always wanted me to work side by side with him. He was so efficient at the job it was amazing. Captain arranged for us to work the same days, so we always worked together. He was a real pro. The first thing he taught me was to never look up at the inmate I was serving. He said, "Jack, if you look up before you put food on his tray, he will eventually accuse you of giving one of your friends more and him less. It will cause you a lot of trouble. Just don't look up, and they can never accuse you of that." It was the best piece of advice I was ever given while working in the kitchen.

One day when I was cleaning chili out of a pot, I got a tap on the shoulder. To clean chili out of the pot, I had to stand on a milk crate to clean over and into the large pot to scrub the bottom. That was the position I was in when I received the tap on the shoulder. I was almost upside down, so I righted myself and turned around. A white inmate about my same age was standing there. I had seen him in the kitchen several times. Usually he was just walking through. I didn't know who he was or what he did. He wasn't dressed in kitchen like us. He was wearing his khakis.

He stuck out his hand and said, "Hi, I'm David Cook."

I shook his hand and responded, "Hello, I am Jack Phillip. What con I do for you?"

He told me, "Look, I am the clerk for food service. I am going to be leaving here via transfer to Buckner, South Carolina, in a couple of weeks. That's only seventy miles from my home. They are going to need a clerk to replace me. Would you be interested in the job?"

I asked him, "Is it a better job than this?"

He laughed and said, "Any job is better than the one you have. I've been watching you, though, and you've worked and never complained. You've taken a lot of bullshit back here from these guys. That's why I thought you might be good in my job."

I said, "Well, does it pay better?"

He really laughed then and said, "Yes, it does. You will always be paid 10 dollars more each month than the highest-paid cook. You will be paid more than anyone in the kitchen." I knew some of the cooks like Captain made over 125 dollars a month!

I told him, "I am definitely interested."

He said, "Come with me and let's go talk to Mrs. Stewart, the secretary. She's my boss." I knew who she was. She was a nice-looking black female that worked as a secretary in food service. She wore civilian clothes. I didn't even know if she was a BOP employee or not. I found out later she was.

We walked down the hallway to her office, and he knocked on the door. She looked up and motioned for us to come in. We went in, and she smiled and said, "Hello." We both returned the greeting.

David said, "Mrs. Stewart, I believe I have found my replacement for the clerk's job. His name is Jack Phillips."

She said, "Well, good. Nice to meet you, Mr. Phillips. Who is your supervisor?"

I told her, "Mr. House."

She said, "Okay, I'll talk to Mr. House, and when you are working and get caught up on your duties, you go work with Mr. Cook and learn all the ins and outs of the clerk's job. When Mr. Cook leaves, you'll be our clerk, Mr. Phillips." I told her, "Thank you, I would do that," and we left her office.

For the next two weeks, I cleaned gutters but no pots. I still served mainline, but I had four or five hours each day to spend with David Cook. David had an office in a hallway. It was an L-shaped hallway that ran between the kitchen itself and the staff dining hall. The staff had their own dining area and a special inmate cook that prepared all their meals fresh. They ate better than we did. In his office, David had a computer, a printer, two small filing cabinets, a desk, two chairs, and a typewriter. The doors at both ends of the hallway were usually locked, but he could get out by simply knocking on the door. An officer would come unlock the door and let him out. It was a cozy setup.

When Captain found out about my new job opportunity, he was ecstatic. He told me he hated to lose me at mainline, but the clerk's job was the best job in food service. He also told me they had talked to him about being the cook in the staff dining area. I could see why. He was great cook. I told him I thought he should take the job. He did and told me to never eat in the inmate chow hall again. He said, "Jack, I'll cook you lunch and bring it back to you. Me and you are going to eat the same food as the staff." That ended up being the best thing about the job! I was eating the same food the warden was eating.

I trained for about two weeks. Then David said, "Okay, you are on your own. I'm not coming in anymore, and you handle it. If you run into any problems and need me, I will be in my room in Memphis Unit." I never had to send for him. I knew how to do the job. It probably took me twice as long at first as it did him, but before too long, I was only actually working two or three hours a day. I spent a lot more time than that in my office. I could now type my letters to Kara and others instead of writing them.

I kept expecting David to leave any day. One of my jobs was to make up the payroll. He was making $150–160 dollars a month. Even though I was doing his job, he still was getting paid. I was too, but I was only making $12 a month doing my job and his job. I was very glad the day he left. For the rest of my time at FCI Memphis, I made over $150 a month in food service. My family did not have to send me any money, and I could send Kara money if needed (but she was making $300 a month!). We were certainly doing better than most in prison.

We had an Italian immigrant working in food service. He was actually raised in America and spoke perfect English but was not an American citizen. His name was Franco. On Thursdays, he made homemade pizzas from scratch. He worked in the bakery, so he had the giant slide-in ovens similar to those in bakeshops. He was such a good baker the staff allowed him to gather up the ingredients and make his twelve pizzas. The food service administrator often came by my office and ate part of the pizza Franco gave me every Thursday. He sold the other pizzas for a book of stamps each. They were the best pizzas I have ever eaten.

There were also two Cubans who worked in the kitchen. One was a cook, and the other was an orderly that did janitor work. They provided constant entertainment in the kitchen. They had been part of the Mariel Cuban boatlift. They had been in America twenty-three years. They had no release date and had never been convicted of a crime here or in Cuba. They had been incarcerated the entire time. Each year they were given a hearing by people from Washington, DC, and told they would get a letter in two weeks telling them if they would be released or not. Two weeks later they would receive a letter telling them they would be in prison another year until their next hearing. They had come here at eighteen years of age. They were both now approaching forty-two! How they hated America!

As a result, they were determined to steal everything they could get their hands on in the kitchen. The cook was continually in and out of Shu for smoking pot. He said he would never ever quit no matter what they did. The janitor pretended that he couldn't under-stand English, so when they told him to do or not do something, he just acted like he didn't understand them. They were relentless thieves and cellmates.

We didn't have microwaves in our units anymore. They said the inmates had destroyed them in the 1994 riots and they refused to replace them. The inmates just became more innovative. The two Cubans had apprehended two regular irons. They taped them together and wired them into one cord, then they stole pie pans from the kitchen and used them as skillets to cook on the irons. They could make virtually any fried food you could think of on those two irons. They literally ran a diner out or their cell. They lived in Memphis Unit-A.

All an inmate had to do was place his order. I would tell them I wanted a double cheeseburger with lettuce, tomato, onion, and ketchup and mustard. They would ask, "What time?" I would tell them, "On the six-o'clock move." At 6:00 p.m., I would go to the door of their unit and ask for them (we weren't allowed to go into units that weren't ours). They would bring my hot cheeseburger wrapped in sandwich paper and in a brown paper bag with the top folded down. I would give them my eight stamps and go on my way. The burgers and ham-and-cheese sandwiches were great!

Of course, they stole everything they cooked from the kitchen. I once watched the Cuban cook walk across the compound in broad daylight with forty-five pounds of raw meat. He had a twenty-five-pound turkey ham under his smock directly behind his head and two ten-pound rolls of hamburger meat stuck up in the arms of his cooking smock. There were always two guards at the exit door of the kitchen looking for contraband. They randomly patted men down and continually found food on inmates, which they just threw into the nearby garbage can. There was no real punishment. The only time they would be punished was if they were stealing raw eggs and raw meat because they were afraid of the various food poisonings those foods could cause if not stored properly.

Here's how the Cuban did it. He would get four of his Cuban buddies to run interference. He would fill their pocket with vegetables and run all four out at the same time knowing the guards would pat them down and find the vegetables. They would be sticking out of their pockets or bulging in their socks so the officers couldn't miss them. While the officers were relieving them of the vegetables and congratulating themselves on their big bust, the Cuban would slip out right around them carrying forty-five pounds of raw meat. We would line up at the kitchen window to watch. It was simply amazing entertainment.

Chapter 14

On the Legal Front

One day in late January, Paul and Phillip Watson (our former football player and friend), the attorney, decided to drive to Cape Girardeau, Missouri, and look in the files of Sam Nance and Timmy Tisdale to find out what they could learn about their case in Missouri. Cape Girardeau was about a three-hour drive from Memphis.

All the way there, Paul and Phillip talked about the discrepancies and inconsistencies in our case. There was much to talk about. There were two main points of emphasis in taking this trip. First, Nance and Tisdale, the witnesses against Kara and me, had testified they had no deals with the government. We already knew they had both received a Rule 35b after our sentencing. We also knew they had received sentence reductions with each Rule 35b. We knew they had immunity because they were not prosecuted for the crime they admitted they committed. Paul and Phillip would look for any trace of a deal they might have had before our trial. Any hint of a deal after their testimony of no deal and the AUSA's continued claim that they had no deal with the government at trial and at sentencing would result in Kara and me being released from jail. There was always the possibility the government could try us again, but Phillip thought that would be unlikely. This was an important trip. Phillip also told Paul he seriously doubted they would find any hint of a deal in their folders in the clerk's office at the Federal Building at Cape Girardeau, Missouri. It wasn't that Phillip doubted they had a deal, for he believed and knew they most certainly did. He just doubted they would be stupid enough to have put it in writing and leave it in their files.

Secondly, they both testified they had never been arrested. Tisdale had once admitted to me he had been arrested in Caruthersville, Missouri. I think he said he agreed to move out of Caruthersville to avoid being prosecuted for the cocaine. Nance denied he had ever been arrested or convicted of any crime prior to the manufacturing charge in Cape Girardeau, to which he had pled guilty and was now serving time.

When Paul and Phillip entered the court house in Cape Girardeau, they went to the clerk's office and asked to see the files on Nance and Tisdale. The clerk directed them to a semiprivate room, brought the files to them, and laid them on the counter. When Phillip opened the files, the second page in each folder was actually a packet of three pages stapled together. In both cases, it was a proffer agreement between the government, and Nance and Tisdale had each signed their proffer agreements on the same day: October 11, 1997. Since our trial wasn't until August 3–10, 1998, they had signed agreements ten months before our trial. They had lied, and AUSA had lied.

Phillip told Paul, "I can't believe it! I just can't believe it!"

Paul asked him, "Believe what?"

Phillip said, "They lied. They all lied. Terry Descusio, the AUSA, lied to the judge and to the jury about the deals. He lied to Judge Burns when he asked him directly about the deals and the AUSA denied they existed. I heard that myself. I can't believe it. Come on, Coach."

Phillip told the clerk he wanted copies of everything in both file. He said they would be right back. Even though January in Missouri is cold, Phillip was so upset he wanted to walk around the block to calm down. He told Paul he was ashamed to be an attorney. He said he had seen all kinds of corruption in twelve years of being an attorney, but he had never seen such professional misconduct. The fact that this was a federal case even made it more appalling. He said that the AUSA had allowed the two witnesses to perjure themselves over and over and over again by testifying they did not have a deal with the government. He told Paul he wished he had never gone to law school.

They also discovered that Nance had multiple prior arrests, again countering his trial testimony. He had been involved in manufacturing meth at least since 1994 and had multiple arrests. They didn't find any convictions. That didn't mean Nance was innocent. They saw reports from the top DEA administrator for Southeast Missouri and Southern Illinois, Howard Herman. Herman had documented cooks and arrests involving Nance in about ten different counties. We would discover later why he had not been convicted of any of those arrests even though it was obvious he was completely guilty. Tisdale had been involved in some of those same cooks.

The second most amazing item Phillip and Paul found in their folders were letters from the federal prosecutor in Nance and Tisdale's case. The AUSA in Cape Girardeau was Hal Prince. The two letters from Prince were to Tisdale's attorney in Sikeston, Missouri, and to Nance's attorney in New Madrid, Missouri. Here is the important part that was found in the identical letters: "I have spoken to Terry Descusio, the AUSA in Memphis, Tennessee. He has guaranteed a deal for your client if he will testify against Jack Phillips."

Although the name was misspelled, it was obvious he meant Jack Phillips—me. This letter was dated May 19, 1998. That would be almost three months *before* our trial.

Now we had proof that Descusio not only lied about the deals but he had guaranteed them himself! Phillip told Paul this was the smoking gun we were looking for. Descusio had not only acted unprofessionally but he had also committed prosecutorial misconduct. Coupled with selective and vindictive prosecution (since he had failed to prosecute Nance, Tisdale, or R. A. Boone), Phillip said, "Paul, Jack, and Kara are going to be fine. They are in great shape."

Paul and Phillip returned to Memphis with the copied files in their possession. I learned what had happened when I called Paul on his cell phone as they were returning. They were both so excited. I had been trying not to be too hopeful. The letdowns were tough. But I will admit, I got excited too. We finally had a break in our case and some real evidence. Those witnesses against us had been bought with the promise of immunity and a reduction in their sentence for their crime in Missouri. It made it a little easier for me to understand why they had lied about Kara and me. It did not make it easier to forgive, just easier to understand.

Phil told me he would come to the prison to visit next week. I had placed him on my visiting list. Of course, he had attorney credentials and could come whenever he wished by simply informing the prison. He showed up during regular visiting hours late on Monday afternoon. It was February 5. He explained everything to me and said he would talk to both Lester and June to bring them up to speed. As he prepared to leave, he said, "Coach, can I do anything else for you right now?"

I said, "Yes, you can. Phillip, would you check on where our motion for a new trial stands? The one that Lester filed in December. I haven' t heard a word, and he won't respond by phone or letter to let me know."

Phillip said he would check on it. He also took the opportunity to ask me why I didn't call him to represent me in the first place. He assured me if I had called him, Kara and I wouldn't be in jail right now. I told him the truth. I told him I had carefully considered doing just that. However, I never felt right about it. I thought a lot of him and trusted him, but I just didn't want to put the responsibility of our lives on him. I loved him. We were like family. I really didn't want to put him in that position. Phillip left, and I went back to the unit.

Three days later, on Thursday, February 8, I was called to the visiting room for an attorney visit in the middle of the afternoon. I assumed it was Lester, but when I got to the visiting room, there was Phillip. We were escorted into a private little office off the visiting room. There were windows, but we could close the door and have complete privacy to talk. We shook hands and sat down. Phillip got up and stepped out to get a cup of coffee out of a machine and asked me if I wanted anything. I told him to grab me a Mountain Dew.

When he returned, he started out by saying, "Listen, Coach, I did check on your motion. It was denied January thirty-first. Now, I have stayed up all night and written this new motion. Here's what

I want you to do. First, sign this paper firing Lester and this other document hiring me as your attorney. I'm not going to charge you anything, Coach, so don't worry about any money. We have until 5:00 p.m. tomorrow afternoon to file this motion." He handed it to me. It was entitled, "A Motion to Reconsider the Motion Previously Filed for a New Trial." Phillip said, "Look through it, and if there is anything we need to change, let's change it." I read through it and made some changes and some minor suggestions.

Phillip said, "Look, Coach, I have found a very remote statute to file this under. I don't even know if it will work or not. You can see I have attached all the exhibits from what we got out of their files in Missouri, and except for the thirteen affidavits from Mason, these are all documents we got in Missouri." He told me to call him early Friday evening.

I thanked Phillip. He gave me all his phone numbers—office, home, cell—and told me not to call until after 5:00 p.m. I made that call, and my hope was restored.

Chapter 15

Communicating with Kara

In reading the Bureau of Prison policy, I found that spouses and immediate family members should be able to write directly to one another. We had been sending letters to Paul, and he would put them in envelopes and address them and mail them to each of us from his house with his return address on the envelope. The catch was we had to get permission. I asked my counselor, Mr. Wren, about it. He called me in a week later and gave me a permission letter to complete. Kara had to do the same thing at her institution. In just a few days, we had permission to write directly to each other. I had continued the practice of writing letters to Kara seven days a week.

I was also able to offer her encouragement about the steps being taken in our legal situation. Paul had already told her, but I was able to write in depth and answer her questions that she had about things. I even copied Phil's motion and mailed her a copy of that. We also sent June Riley a copy since she was by record still Kara's attorney. We also sent each other a commissary sheet from our institution to compare prices and goods that each institution offered.

There were also policies regarding telephone calls. Inmates that were husbands and wives or sons and daughters or brothers and sisters were normally allowed one phone call each quarter (for a total of four a year). However, it was totally at the discretion of the warden. Of course, the unit team would have some say in the warden's decision. They would have to set up and monitor such phone calls. It meant more work for them, and they didn't want to do any work, much less additional optional work. It required a lot of organization to place calls. Times would have to be set in both institutions, places for the phone calls, and staff to monitor the calls. It would take several phone calls or faxes just to set up the inmate phone calls.

Kara's unit team and warden agreed to our phone calls. I was simply told, "No way, Phillips. We don't allow any incoming or outgoing inmate to inmate calls from this institution." They told me I could file a grievance if I didn't like it, but I knew it was futile to file a grievance to those who had caused the grievance.

We could have resorted to the old setup Paul had at home, but if they construed that as a three-way call, we would lose our writing privileges, all our other phone calls, and possibly visitation days or even good time credit. We couldn't risk it.

I wouldn't get to talk to Kara again until 2003 (it was still 1999).

Chapter 16

Perry, Lionel, and Mitch

There were so many interesting characters at FCI Memphis. It was not so different than regular society. There were kinds in that population. Two of the men, Perry and Lionel, were both men that attended my Bible-study class.

Perry was a small older black man, probably in his early fifties. He had been a drug addict most of his life and was doing a short prison sentence for possession of drugs. Perry couldn't read or write at all. An amazing thing happened to him one night in our Bible study. We read a lot of scripture in that Bible-study group. Paul let his students in his public school classroom donate money in a jar on his desk to purchase Bibles. Paul allowed them to donate the money only when he was not in the classroom or when he could not see. When we needed Bibles in our group, he would purchase what we needed and send them to us. He posted small little Bible-like decals for every Bible they bought along the edge of the whiteboard in his class. It didn't take long to cover the entire edge of the whiteboard with those little decaled Bibles. Perry was given one of those Bibles. We always looked up the Bible passage for Him and told him what verses we were on and encouraged him to follow along. He always tried.

After about a month of Bible study, the amazing event occurred. Perry, with tears streaming down his face, looked up one night and said, "Mr. Coach, I can read! I read all the words you are saying. Let me read the next one." I let him go ahead and read the next verse. He read it correctly! After that, we always let Perry read the first verse. In some way, he had learned to read. It was miraculous.

After only a few months, Perry had his unit team meeting. In that meeting, they told him he was approaching his release date. When he told us at Bible study, we all cheered. Perry didn't even smile. As the day for his release grew near, Perry became more and more agitated. He stuck around the cell the night before he was supposed to leave and said he wanted to talk to me.

Perry wept and sobbed as he told me he didn't want to leave. He had no family in Memphis and no real friends. He had nowhere to go. He doubted he could read well enough to even take the driver's license test and pass it. He had no skills. He had never had a steady job. His future out there, he said, was to be alone and homeless and hungry. He confided that he would prefer to just stay with us right there in prison. He had food, medical care, shelter, friends, and our Bible study.

Perry stayed in my room for almost two hours. I saw him as he was leaving the next day. He was still weeping. He bugged me real hard and said, "Mr. Coach, I don't want to go!" My heart hurt for him. Two months later, Perry was back on a probation violation. He was smiling from ear to ear as he entered the unit. For Perry, prison was home, and he was glad to be back.

Lionel was a sturdy-built black man in his mid- to late twenties. He was in prison for bank robbery. He transferred to FCI Memphis from some other institution a few months after I arrived. He and another young black man had been put up to robbing a bank in a small Mississippi town. Like many small towns in the South, it had a court square, which meant there was a courthouse and a street shaped like a square around it with stores opposite the courthouse on all four sides. The bank was one of these stores. Lionel and the other youngster were recruited to rob this bank by an older man. The plan was that he would let them out, drive around the courthouse until they came out, pick them up, and make their getaway out of town.

However, while they were in the bank with gun drawn and robbing the place, a county deputy parked at the courthouse right across from the bank. The man driving the car was frightened by this and decided to just drive on out of town. Lionel and the other man came out of the bank with a gun in one hand and a bag of money in the other. They waited for the man to drive by and pick them up. He never came. After a few minutes, several officers came out of the courthouse with their guns drawn and captured the two bank robbers.

I asked Lionel why he didn't just run when the driver failed to show up. He said, "Mr. Jack, I didn't even know what town we was in. I didn't know which way to run."

Lionel was finally assigned a job to take care of the floors in the dining area of the food service department. After I became the clerk, I had the officer wake me up Monday to Friday at 4:30 a.m. instead of 3:00 a.m. I usually left for work near 6:00 a.m. Every day I left, Lionel would be sitting in the dayroom in his white kitchen clothes watching television. He was assigned a shift that ran from 8:00 a.m. until 3:30 p.m. When the dining room supervisor took roll right after the 8:00 a.m. move had closed, Lionel was never there. About the fourth day in a row that that happened, she said she was going to put him in the Shu (also called the hole). I pulled her aside after count that day, and I told the dining room supervisor that Lionel could not tell time. I told her he was always up and dressed and ready to go by 6:00 a.m. He really didn't mind working. I told her if she didn't tell him to leave at 3:30 p.m., chances are he would stay there and end up being locked in the dining hall during 4:00 count. He didn't know when to come or when to leave. She could hardly believe it.

I told her if she would find someone working the same hours as Lionel and send him by Beale-B unit to get him, he would never be late for work. And if she had the same inmate walk him back to the unit at 3:30 p.m., he would always be gone on time. She was skeptical, but she did agree to try it. Lionel was never late for work again.

One night before Bible study as Keith and I were just sitting in our cell, there was a light knock on the door. It was Lionel. I told him it wasn't time for Bible study yet, but he said he needed to come in right now. We told him to come on in. He reached into his shirt pocket and pulled out two long, fat cigars (in looking at him, I had noticed he must have had a dozen cigars in his shirt pocket). He walked over to us and said, "Here's one for you, Coach, and one for you, Mr. Keith."

Keith and I both looked at each other, and finally, Keith said, "What's this for, Lionel?"

He said "I'm a new dad. My wife just had a baby boy this afternoon." He smiled like a really proud poppa. He was a happy, proud new dad.

I knew he had been down for several years before he transferred to FCI Memphis, so I said, "Lionel, can I ask you something?"

He said, "Sure."

I asked him, "Haven't you been down four or five years?"

He said, "Yes, sir."

I then said, "Lionel, I hope I'm not being too personal, but how did your wife get pregnant if you have been locked up four or five years?"

He just looked at me matter-of-factly and said, "We had phone sex."

I looked at Keith and he looked at me. We were trying to decide if he was just kidding us or not. We both realized he was not kidding! His wife had convinced him she had become pregnant by talking about sex with him on the telephone. I guess it is true: what you don't know won't hurt you!

There is no doubt in my mind that both Perry and Lionel were mentally retarded to some degree. There was a large number of mentally ill and mentally challenged people in that facility.

That wasn't the case with Mitch, a fat white man from St. Louis, about forty years old, with a high school education, and could read anything. He didn't have a job even though everyone was supposed to work. Mitch rarely left the unit except to eat and seemed to in the unit all the time. He never attended our Bible study.

His claim to fame was that he stayed up every night and listened to Art Bell on *Coast to Coast* on the radio. He spent all day the next day trying to tell you all he had heard. *Coast to Coast* similar to the *National Inquirer*, except on radio. Alien sightings and abductions, UFO sightings, Bigfoot sightings, and every weird subject you can imagine made up the broadcasts. The more bizarre it was, the more likely it was to make the show. Their audience was committed and just as strange as the show. Keith and I would often make up elaborate stories and asked him if he heard that the night before on *Coast to Coast* like we had. He would always say, "Yeah, I heard that." We realized he wasn't actually staying up and listening every night. He was sleeping most of the night just like we were.

The reason Mitch is even worth discussing is because of his fascination with urinology. If you are not familiar with that term, it refers to drinking your own urine in order to gain multiple benefits. Mitch had ordered at least three books to support his new lifestyle. He claimed it cured cancer, Ebola, E. coli, AIDS, and many other deadly diseases. As a result, each morning you would see Mitch carrying around a mug of his own urine and drinking every drop of it. The old crusty inmate, Morgan, often told Mitch, "Hey, Mitch, Phillips and I both have to take a piss. How would you like a mixed drink this morning."

"No!"

"Well, how about a shit sandwich to go with your mug of urine?"

Mitch was disgusting. Keith eventually banned him from entering our cell. He was extremely overweight and had a roll of fat across his middle. When he sweated, he always sweated along the top of the roll of fat around his middle. It was always yellow, the same color of urine. He also smoked two or three packs of cigarettes a day. He died two years later of undetermined natural causes.

Chapter 17

A Violent Place

There was never a doubt about this being an extremely violent place. The first time I went to the laundry room, all the washing machines were in use. I placed my laundry bag on top of one running machine and checked the time on the machine to see when I needed to come back and put my laundry in.

After I came back and washed my clothes, I had to wait for a dryer. I set my bag of washed clothes on top of the second dryer. I was ready to go in next. When I returned about thirty minutes later, I grabbed the bag on the second dryer and started emptying the clothes into the empty dryer. Suddenly, there was a very loud clanging noise as the clothes tumbled into the dryer. I reached in the dryer and pulled out a sixteen-inch to eighteen-inch shiv (a large knife, this was more like a sword) out of the dryer. The metal was sharpened fine, and it was so large it could easily go completely through the body of a man. It had a sturdy handle on it as well. I was shocked and wondered how that got into my laundry bag. I wondered if someone was trying to set me up to get me in trouble.

As I looked more carefully, I realized that bag of clothes was not my laundry bag of clothes! I searched around and found my clothes in another dryer. I reached in the second dryer and got a washcloth and wiped down the shiv because it now had my fingerprints on it. I then placed the other person's clothes I had pulled out of the second dryer back in that dryer.

Almost everyone had a knife or weapon. At one point, I even saw a zip gun, which is a homemade gun that would shoot .22-caliber bullets. I even saw a .22-caliber bullet in an inmate's locker. It was such a violent place people were almost paranoid to try to defend and protect themselves. There were probably a dozen stabbings I knew that happened.

Fights on the compound were also common. These were unlike the school yard fights I had witnessed. Some were really fights to the death had they been allowed to continue. Why did they fight as if their life depended on it? Because their life did depend upon winning. The officers never rushed in to break up a fight. They were afraid too. When they had overwhelming numbers (and I mean overwhelming numbers), then and only then would the officers rush in to break up a fight.

There was a fight one day during the noonday meal. The two inmates calmly walked into the center of the compound right out in the open, and the fight was on. They were both about 6 feet 2 inches and 240 pounds. They were everyday weight lifters and big and strong with no fat. They were evenly matched, so when they started, they began throwing haymakers. I mean take-your-head-off-your-shoulders punches. I have never seen heavier blows than those two men threw and landed on each other. Both had on their institutional boots, khaki pants, and white T-shirts. It wasn't long until they were both bleeding profusely and the T-shirts had been torn off. Both were covered in blood. One man would get knocked down, then he would get up and knock the other man down. The blows were brutal. They must have landed 200 punches apiece, and they were all power punches. Their ability to absorb those blows and keep fighting was amazing. They were really tough men, so neither could gain an advantage. About twenty guards finally rushed the men and put them on the ground by the force of their momentum charging in. The men just relaxed and allowed the officers to handcuff them and take them to the Shu.

After the fights, the issue was usually over. They settled their differences most of the time with their fists. Normally, the violent attacks were decisive because one was the winner. Occasionally the fights, like the stabbings, resulted in a trip to the nearby hospital. While I was at FCI Memphis, there was not a death from a fistfight.

Fights were so normal the officers didn't panic. The men that fought were usually out of the hole within forty-eight hours unless a weapon was used. Fighting there was just part of the culture. We had the Vice Lords, the Gangster Disciples, and other gangs on the compound. The groups had a workable truce. One group handled the alcohol, another the gambling, and still another the drugs and other contraband. Those two major gangs had pushed the lesser gangs into an almost underground role.

One of the main places fights occurred was in the line for meals at the chow hall. Everyone wanted to eat as fast as possible to get the warmest and best food. If I wanted to fight, all I had to do was go to the chow line and cut in line. You could be sure if someone cut line, someone else (or many others) would take offense. It always resulted in a fight or stabbing. A man in a wheelchair once cut across and in front of a man between the main serving line and the hot bar. It was taking the man at the regular line a little extra time to get his food because the servers had to change pans. The man in the wheelchair had had his tray handed over the line to him, so he just went around the man in front and was ready to use the hot bar. Bad mistake. The man turned around and saw the man in the wheelchair had cut in front of him, so he just dumped the food off his tray on the floor, walked around the side of the man in the wheelchair until he was in front, then turned and knocked the man in the wheelchair backward out of his chair. The man then jumped on him and in just a few seconds beat him unconscious. The officers came over and pulled him off the unconscious man.

The officers asked him why he hit the man in the wheelchair like that. He simply said, "He cut in front of me." The guards just nodded. They closed the compound and handcuffed him and took him to the hole. He was released the next day. The guards believed and understood his story. Respect was important. The man in the wheelchair had to go to the hospital. He was gone six days. He never cut in line again.

I only had one problem in the violence area while I was there. It happened during early-morning short line (meal for kitchen workers). I got into it with a young gangbanger from Philadelphia. I don't remember what started it, but I turned my tray sideways and hit him across the bridge of his nose before he could hit me. It broke his nose. It seemed as if his nose just exploded and blood went everywhere. Whatever the details, I know I had no choice. I had to fight, or so I determined. I just hit him first. I probably had no chance to win the fight unless I did that. The first blow dropped him to his knees. The fight was over. He raised his hands and said, "Okay, Coach! That's enough. You broke my nose." From that day on, he and I became really good friends. I can't explain that.

It seemed like Keith was always having someone wanting to jump on him. He would do a lot of mouthing off to everybody. Sometimes he would cross that imaginary line. I walked around the comer in education one day and saw a large black man grab Keith by the neck and lift him up about two feet off the ground and pin him to the wall. The man was threatening to kill Keith. I talked him into putting Keith down, but before he would, he wanted Keith to apologize. I had to talk Keith into apologizing. He didn't want to. They finally agreed to let it go and forget about it. Oftentimes Keith was misunderstood, but many times he just pushed too far. They thought he was making fun of them or talking down to them. In some cases, Keith was doing that or both or something entirely different. Keith had to learn where to draw the line and stop.

Chapter 18

Education

Keith got a job tutoring math in education in the GED classes and working with the vocational officer. I submitted so many copouts and had heard nothing, but they hired Keith.

In April, 1999, one of the volunteers sent word to me in food service to come talk to him. I went to education and had a conversation with him. He wanted me to come over one day to his class and lecture them on anything in relation to social studies / history. His classes met from 8:00 a.m.–10:00 a.m. and the second class from 1:00 p.m.–3:00 p.m. I told him I would love to but I would have to speak with my boss, Mrs. Stewart, the secretary in food service. She said it was fine with her as long as I got my work finished before I went.

I went to the 8:00 a.m. class on Tuesday the next week. There were about twenty-five men in that GED class. I watched him try to give them a worksheet to do before I started my lecture. He laid a workbook on their desk, and they just knocked it to the floor and continued talking to their neighbor. They totally disrespected this seventy-two-year-old volunteer. They weren't in class because they wanted to be. They were required by law to attend class if they had no high school diploma. If they refused, they could and would lose their good time credit.

I had decided to lecture about how we had gotten involved in Vietnam and to explain the difficulties we had in that conflict from a political point of view. I didn't have any notes, but I didn't need any because I had lived through that period of time and knew the details intimately. As I began talking, about ten men in the back of the room just ignored me and continued talking (out loud) to one another. I just laid down my chalk and said, "I'm not doing this. I am not trying to talk over you."

Several of the inmates that had been listening peaked up. They turned around and told those men, "Shut up! We asked Coach to come talk to us, and we want to hear him. You be respectful, or we'll come back there and beat your ass." They turned back around and told me, "Go ahead, Coach, we want to hear this."

I lectured that day and went back on Thursday to lecture again. The reception was great that day. I lectured on the details of World War II and talked almost two straight hours. The men all shook my hand when I finished and said they loved it and hoped I would come back again.

That same afternoon, I was called over the intercom to report to education. I told Mrs. Stewart, and she told me to go on over. I went there and was ushered into Mrs. Crawford's office. She was a staff member classified as a teacher and was in charge of the GED classroom that I had lectured. The assistant supervisor of education and another staff member were also in the office. All three were females.

Mrs. Crawford said, "Well, Mr. Phillips, what's it going to take to hire you to work in education? We've heard nothing but good reports about your teaching from the men in that class. They loved you."

I said, "Mrs. Crawford, I don't think you can afford me." I knew Keith was only making about $35 a month.

She said, "What do you make as the clerk in the kitchen?"

I told her, "I made $160 last month."

She said, "Well, I couldn't pay that. I could only pay you about $35 a month."

I told them, "My wife is locked up too. I need the money I make. I would be glad to tutor some of the men at night or continue lecturing or help in any way I can. I'm a teacher. I would teach for free because I just love teaching. I don't want to lose my teaching skills. I can't understand why you didn't hire me three months ago after I put in cop-outs and even had an interview with Mrs. Jones."

She said, "We'd like to have you in education. Let me see what we can work out."

I said, "Okay," shook hands with them all, left, and went back to work at food service.

About 3:15 p.m. they called me back to education again. I went straight to Mrs. Crawford's office. She said, "We have a proposal. We would like to give you eight men who have been in our program for years and haven't made any progress in a while. They are older, good men and won't give you any trouble. We would like to give you those men as a GED class. You would teach them from 1:00 p.m.–3:00 p.m. on Monday, Wednesday, and Friday. You will also teach them from 6:00 p.m.–8:00 p.m. on Tuesday and Thursdays. All eight of the men have agreed to those times, and we will have a room open for you to use. What do you say?"

I said, "I'll have to check all this out with Mrs. Stewart. Those afternoon hours are part of my workday, but I can tell you I would like to do it." I really didn't even know what they taught in the GED program, but I knew I could do it. If I had any trouble with the math, I would get Keith to help me or teach it to my students himself.

She said, "Well, we can't pay you because you are getting paid another job, but we can give you a twenty-five-dollar bonus each month for your work."

I told her, "I will let you know tomorrow morning after I talk to Mrs. Stewart." We left it at that. Of course, Mrs. Stewart agreed as long as I did my work in food service. I began teaching GED while still functioning as the food service clerk. Seven of those eight men in my class got their GED in the next six months. FCI Memphis lead the BOP nation in the number of graduates that year with 148. There were about 100 institutions that had GED programs. I was never paid the $25 bonus the entire time I taught in education at FCI Memphis.

Chapter 19

Hope in Court

In April, we received the news for which we had been waiting: Phillip's motion had worked! Judge Burns had granted the motion and set a date for an evidentiary hearing to present newly discovered evidence. The date he set was July 26, 1999. July 27 was my birthday and also our anniversary. The best scenario was to win the hearing and be set free too celebrate our twenty-ninth anniversary together! We were extremely excited. It could actually happen.

We were confident because we had documentation that Terry Descusio, the AUSA, had offered Tisdale and Nance deals before our trial. He had lied about it at trial in front of the judge and jury and lied again at the sentencing hearing directly to Judge Burn's face in his answer to Judge Burn's direct question. With the information I had gained using the Freedom of Information Act and the information Paul and Phillip had gotten in Missouri, we had documentation that Nance and Tisdale had lied under the oath about their previous arrests. All that goes to their credibility. We also had deals they had signed and lied about, plus we also still had the thirteen men who had signed the affidavits.

With all the evidence we had, I felt like Descusio could be disbarred for all the misconduct he was guilty of, including lying to the judge and misrepresenting the truth to the jury. I also was sure Nance and Tisdale's testimony would finally be labeled as perjured. Phillip even felt like we would win. He believed if we won the right to a new trial on those grounds with the issues we were raising, the government would not want to put us on trial again. Judge Burns also instructed us to submit a list of anyone we wanted to subpoena for the hearing.

I began compiling a list. Naturally, we wanted Nance and Tisdale there. We also subpoenaed the thirteen inmates who had submitted affidavits. These men were now scattered from Tennessee and Illinois to Florida, Alabama, Texas, Mississippi, Arkansas, and even California. It was going to cost the government to transport and house all those men. We also asked for a subpoena for Mike Fields, who was housed in federal lockup in Marion, Illinois. We didn't know what he knew, but we wanted to find that out if possible. There was some reason the government hadn't called him as a witness after transporting him to Mason, Tennessee, for our trial. The judge approved them all. He guaranteed us he would be available to be called as witnesses at our hearing on July 26, 1999.

All the inmates I talked to at FCI Memphis were astounded. To the man, they all said this never happened. It was unheard of that a convicted man in the feds would get an evidentiary hearing after he had been convicted. They felt like we had a great chance of gaining our freedom.

About 50 percent of the men at FCI Memphis thought they would probably die in prison while serving out their long sentences. As a result, those inmates *demanded* respect from inmates and staff alike, and they got it. The staff said, "Do you mind doing this or that?" or "Would you do this or that?" It was never, "Do this or that!" If a staff member wanted to start a riot, all he had to do was denigrate any inmate there. That was understood by staff and inmate alike.

We all kept working on the case. We were accumulating more and more evidence. We were eager for July to hurry get here! We had a great chance to win and go home and end the nightmare.

Because it was spring, our softball season was just about to begin. I was going to experience softball competition in prison. There were four teams, and we were the second or third best team, but it was competitive enough that any team could beat any other. I began playing shortstop and then third, but I had arm problems that lasted all summer and ended up playing first base. I hadn't played competitive baseball or softball in about twenty years. Slow-pitch softball looked easier than it was. I was always able place hit ball wherever wanted it to go, but it still took me half the summer to become an effective hitter. Paul continued to provide books for Kara and me, and I worked hard at both my jobs. The clerk job was easy now, and I began to understand what was on the GED and how I needed to teach it. Paul also continued copying Bible studies for me, and our group was growing and maturing. The church at FCI Memphis was functioning like one should. We had a great head chaplain (although some of the inmates tried to take advantage of him and caused him many problems) and outstanding visiting preachers, Bible-study teachers, choirs, and missionaries come in to minister to us. Some famous Memphis musicians came in weekly to play and sing to the men in the Shu and on the compound. They had been coming for decades, and it was not publicized because they are still coming today as far as I know. You would be surprised. They are some of the biggest names ever in Memphis music.

I was adjusting to my incarceration but still had those panic attacks at the thought of being away from all I loved. Kara had made a few friends, had a good job at UNICOR, and seemed to be safe, but I knew she was lonely too. She was farther away from home and had fewer visits than me. Her letters really lifted my spirits when I saw the little-colored envelope at mail call each day. Paul and Jen still visited weekly. They brought Mom and Dad as often as they could considering both had serious health issues. Dad was now in a wheelchair full-time. They were living, more or less, at Paul's house. I always enjoyed their visits. Keith's mom began coming to visit him at the same time Paul and Jen came. So usually it would be Paul and Jen, Morgan and me, and Keith and his mom visiting together in the visiting room.

Our daughter, Mary Lynn, and the grandkids came to visit too. Our son, Carey, even came a time or two, but he just couldn't handle seeing Kara or me incarcerated. Kara's visits were even more rare because Mary Lynn and her family just couldn't afford to go too often. Paul often went with them or helped with the expense. Carey got upset one Christmas and tried to get someone to go with him to see his mom in Texas. None of them could go, so he called a friend to go with him, and they just took off to Texas to visit Kara. It just killed him to see us locked up and then have to leave us there.

Chapter 20

Byron Smith and Ricky Short

In early April, Ricky Short and his new wife had come to visit. Her name was Vicky, and she managed some apartments in her hometown in Alabama. She also had a thirteen-year-old daughter from a previous relationship.

Vicky was an attractive blonde. Ricky had met her at a casino in Tunica, Mississippi. He had sent me a picture of them together. I was surprised when I met her. I could tell she was flirting with me. I had no idea why.

About a week after their visit, Paul came to see me. He had a call from the real estate agent that owned the house where we had lived. The same house where Byron and Ricky had continued living after our incarceration. I knew Byron had taken a job driving a truck. I didn't know Ricky had packed up completely and moved to Alabama. The agent said the rent hadn't been paid since March. He wanted Paul to get our stuff out of the house.

Paul said he, his son Abel, and my son Carey would move our stuff out by Tuesday the next week. He said he would store it in his garage and in a storage room he already had rented. I thought that was a good idea.

When I talked to him on Thursday, all the moving had been completed and everything was out of the house. Much to my surprise, Ricky and Byron had apparently looted our possessions. All our small kitchen items—microwave, toaster, even the refrigerator— were gone. My large-screen TV and smaller bedroom TV were also gone. Our telephones, clocks, coffee and end tables, and other miscellaneous items were also missing. Paul wasn't sure what else was gone because he didn't know exactly what we had.

Paul had to remove all our clothes, pictures, bedroom suites, bedroom furniture, my desk, dishes, and items stored in closets and in the attic. It was a really sad week for me. When I thought about *going home*, I thought about returning to 711 Highway 72. Now it was just an empty house. It was no longer our home. Mary Lynn had taken the car and picked up the payments. Kara and I no longer had a home or a car to return to. It seemed another chapter of our lives was quickly closing.

Later I received a letter from Ricky Short. He had sent along some more photos of his new wife and her daughter. In the photos, I could see my coffee table and three remotes that ran the TV and accompanying electronic devices. Then I noticed a round end table my grandmother had given Laura and me on our anniversary. The more I looked, I recognized the distinctive corner of my large screen television!

Seeing the remotes and the television was a shock. Ricky had told Paul he had stored the TV and my large appliances in a large building that housed his brother's pallet company. I knew the building had been in it. Ricky told Paul someone had broken into the building and stolen the television and the larger appliances he had been keeping for me. Betrayal by a friend is one of the deepest hurts. I would have given Ricky all those things had he just asked. Instead, he had lied and stolen them from us. I imagined all my other missing items had gone the same way.

Over the next few months I heard Ricky and Vicky had divorced. I was told by a friend later that Ricky was blaming me for his divorce. He had always had Vicky write letters to me. He would tell her what to say, and she would do the writing. In answering one of those letters, I told Vicky to ask Ricky about my television. I guess this was the part I played in causing their divorce. I never heard from either of them again. I surmised he had gotten money from Vicky to supposedly "buy" the television and had pocketed the money instead. Ricky loved the casinos and loved to gamble. I think Vicky realized Ricky had conned her out of several hundred dollars. The chapter of my life that had intersected with Ricky Short and Byron South had ended.

Chapter 21

Evidentiary Hearing, Morning, July 26, 1999

July 1999 had finally arrived. We had been waiting for July ever since Judge Burns had granted Phillip's motion and we had been granted an evidentiary hearing. For the first time since our legal battle began, we were really prepared. July 6, we had celebrated the first birthday of our youngest granddaughter, Michelle. Also, on the twenty-seventh of July, I would celebrate my forty-eighth birthday, and Kara and I would celebrate our twenty-ninth wedding anniversary. However, today it was July 26, 1999, the date of our hearing.

Keith and I were both taken to R and D since he would testify in my hearing. We were placed in holding cells around 6:00 a.m. Keith was placed in one cell, and I in another cell. Much to my surprise, Brent Frazier, the young man that had first run up to me at Mason after our conviction, was in the same cell I was placed in. He was waiting to go to court with us. We had his affidavit as well. I didn't know where he had come from.

He had a surprise for me. He asked that we not call him as a witness. He told me he had cut a deal with the government and had testified against some other people for a sentence reduction in his case (just like Nance and Tisdale had done in ours). He told me his dad was afraid it might jeopardize his deal and against the government. I explained to him we had already used his affidavit when we filed the motion. He knew that and didn't mind it; he just didn't want to testify. He was afraid the government would retaliate if he did. This is intimidating a witness, a prime example of that illegal activity. I just told him I would pass it along to my attorney, Phillip Watson.

Arriving at the federal building was like a Mason reunion. All thirteen of the men from whom we had obtained affidavits at Mason were there. I met one man they brought in from California. I had never met him before. He had lived in the dorm with Nance and Tisdale and had sent along his written statement to me without us ever having met. He had given a sworn affidavit to Phillip at Mason earlier, and then he'd been transferred to California. There were other men in the holding cells too. They were, for the most part, in court for other cases. I would later learn that one of those men was Mike Fields, Brent Frazier's old cellmate from Mason who had been brought in for our trial but was never used in court. He no longer had a beard, and his hair was much shorter than the last time I had seen him.

The hearing was set to start at 9:00 a.m. I wished Kara could have been there. It was in this very courthouse that I had last seen her. I was taken into the court at 8:55 a.m. Phillip Watson was there, and we shook hands. He smiled and said, "This is going to be a good day, Coach."

I said, "Good!"

Before we could say much more, the court was called to order, and the hearing began.

The judge said he wanted to hear from Phillip and from the AUSA, Terry Descusio, regarding the issues in our filed brief. Phillip laid his cards on the table. He said, "Your Honor, we can now prove that the two primary witnesses against Jack and Kara Phillips lied about their arrest record. We will further prove that Mr. Descusio lied to the court at trial and to you at sentencing. I was in court the day of sentencing, although not the attorney, and I myself heard Mr. Descusio outright lie at least three times. The conviction of my client and his wife is the clear result of the lies told by the two government witnesses and the AUSA."

Descusio was fuming. He roared as he jumped out of his seat, "Your Honor, I have been an Assistant United States Attorney for twenty-six years. I have never been called a liar in court. I resent my reputation being smeared by Mr. Watson! I resent that he has called me liar over and over here today already, and we've just started."

The judge looked at Phillip and said, "Well, Mr. Watson?"

Phil went into his country-bumpkin routine and hemmed and hawed around and finally said, "Your Honor, he's not a liar . . . no, he's a damn liar."

The AUSA was on his feet in a flash. However, the judge intervened. He said, "That's enough, Mr. Watson. The court understands that you believe the AUSA has lied in this case. Now, let's get on with it and see if you can prove it. Call your first witness." Phillip called Sam Nance.

Mr. Watson: Mr. Nance, I am Phillip Watson. I am Mr. Jack Phillip's attorney. I only want to ask you a few questions this morning. First, did you testify at the Phillips trial that you had no deal with the government?

Mr. Nance: I did.

Mr. Watson: Did you or did you not receive a Rule 35b and a significant reduction in your sentence on your case in Missouri for your testimony in the Phillips trial?

Mr. Nance: Yeah, but that was after the trial. That doesn't mean I had a deal before.

Mr. Watson: Please just answer the question, Mr. Nance. We don't need all the commentary. Did you get prosecuted for the meth lab in Memphis?

Mr. Nance: No.

Mr. Watson: Then you must have had immunity. Isn't that a deal, Mr. Nance?

Mr. Nance: I don't know.

Phillip returned to the defense lawyer's table and pulled out some legal documents. He gave a copy to Descusio and a copy to the clerk. He told the judge, "Your Honor, I would like to place this document into the record as exhibit A. The judge nodded at the clerk and said, "Very well."

Mr. Watson: (He asked the judge if he could approach the witness, and the judge said he could.) Mr. Nance, would you please read the title of this document and the first paragraph?

Mr. Nance: Okay (as he took the document).

Mr. Nance read the document with the title *Proffer Agreement*. In the first paragraph, it clearly stated that it was an agreement with the government that this so-named person (Nance) would be recommended for a sentence reduction if his testimony resulted in the conviction of others.

Mr. Watson: Mr. Nance, what is the date on that proffer agreement?

Mr. Nance: October 13, 1997.

Mr. Watson: So ten months before the Phillips went to trial, you signed this proffer agreement with the government. Mr. Nance, isn't this a deal with the government? Mr. Nance, turn over to page three. Is that your signature, or did someone forge your name?

Mr. Nance: It is my signature.

Mr. Watson: So didn't you really have a deal with the government?

Mr. Nance: Yes.

Mr. Watson: Isn't it also true that you testified that you had never been arrested or convicted of a crime except for the one for which you are now serving time?

Mr. Nance: Yes.

Mr. Watson: Is that your testimony today?

Mr. Nance: Yes.

Mr. Watson: Isn't it true, Mr. Nance, that you have been arrested many times but never convicted?

Mr. Nance: Yes.

Mr. Watson: Arrested by the SEMO Drug Task Force?

Mr. Nance: Yes.

Mr. Watson: Arrested by the Pemiscot County Sheriff's Office?

Mr. Nance: Yes.

Mr. Watson: Arrested by the Dunklin Count Sheriff's Office at least twice? Released once on twenty-five-thousand-dollar bond and again on a twenty-thousand-dollar bond in the same month?

Mr. Nance: Yes.

Mr. Watson: Arrested by the New Madrid County Sheriff's Office?

Mr. Nance: Yes.

Mr. Watson: Arrested by the New Madrid City Police?

Mr. Nance: Yes.

Mr. Watson: Weren't all these charges for manufacturing meth and/or possessing with the intent to deliver meth?

Mr. Nance: Yes.

Mr. Watson: And how much time did you serve on all those charges?

Mr. Nance: None.

Mr. Watson: So you were arrested and won in court and was never convicted, right?

Mr. Nance: Not exactly.

Mr. Watson: Well, what happened with all those arrests?

Mr. Nance: The court records in Missouri were all sealed and closed.

Mr. Watson: So you had at least six arrests in Missouri, seven counting the one you are doing time for, and were responsible for the crime in Memphis in this case? You've only served time for one offense?

Mr. Nance: Yes.

Mr. Watson: Mr. Nance, that is true because you have been a government witness all along and paid for your cooperation. No more questions, Mr. Nance.

Judge Burns: Mr. Descusio, do you have a cross for Mr. Nance?

Mr. Descusio: Uh, yes, I mean . . . just a few follow-up . . . uh . . . questions, Your Honor.

Judge Burns: Very well.

Mr. Descusio: Mr. Nance, you . . . you didn't get your Rule 35b until sometime . . . I mean sometime in December 1998, is that right?

Mr. Nance: That's right.

Mr. Descusio: When you testified at trial, it was . . . it was . . . it was . . . what? August of 1998?

Mr. Nance: Yes.

Mr. Descusio: So if you didn't get your Rule 35b . . . your Rule 35b . . . until December, then you were telling the truth at trial when you said you didn't have a deal, right?

Mr. Watson: Objection, Your Honor, the AUSA knows from our exhibit A that Mr. Nance had a deal as early as October 1997. Furthermore, we don't know what previous deals he had from all those other arrests in 1994, 1995, and 1996 in Missouri, where the records are all sealed and closed. Mr. Nance certainly had a deal before the trial in August 1998.

Judge Burns: Sustained. Mr. Descusio, rephrase your question.

Mr. Descusio: Never mind, Your Honor. No more questions for the witness.

Mr. Nance was excused from the stand. It was obvious this time he had not been prepped like the last time. He had also not been groomed to look like the boy next door. He looked like what he really was, a convict through and through. Phillip then called Timmy Tisdale to the stand. He admitted he too had lied about having a deal. Phillip went through the same routine on the proffer agreement as he had with Nance. The agreements were identical. Tisdale admitted he had lied in court, but he did point out he had said he hoped to get something for his testimony. Phillip went to work on him then.

Mr. Watson: Yes, you did say that at trial. But you also said, and I quote, "I don't have a deal with anybody." Didn't you say that in front of the jury, Mr. Tisdale, or would you like me to show you the transcript?

Mr. Tisdale: No, I said it.

Mr. Watson: Didn't you say you had never been arrested or convicted before your current offense?

Mr. Tisdale: Yes.

Mr. Watson: Is that still your testimony?

Mr. Tisdale: Well, I was arrested once for marijuana in 1992 and once for cocaine in Caruthersville, Missouri, in 1993, but I was never convicted.

Mr. Watson: Your Honor, I would like to enter this proffer agreement between the US government and Mr. Tisdale into the record as exhibit B.

Judge Burns: So be it.

Mr. Watson: Mr. Tisdale, would you read the title and first paragraph of this document I am handing you?

Mr. Tisdale: Okay.

Mr. Watson: Would you turn to page three of the document? Now, sir, is that your signature, or did someone forge your name?

Mr. Tisdale: No, that's my signature.

Mr. Watson: What is the date by your name?

Mr. Tisdale: October 13, 1997.

Mr. Watson: Do you recall testifying at the trial against Jack and Kara Phillips?

Mr. Tisdale: Yes, it was in the summer.

Mr. Watson: Does August of 1998 sound about right?

Mr. Tisdale: Yes.

Mr. Watson: Is it safe to say, Mr. Tisdale, that your testimony at that trial that you did not have a deal is accurate?

Mr. Tisdale: No, it was not accurate.

Mr. Watson: No more questions, Your Honor.

Judge Burns: Cross, Mr. Descusio?

Mr. Descusio: No questions, Your Honor.

Judge Burns: The ball is back in your court, Mr. Watson.

Phillip told the judge that the existence of these two documents, exhibits A and B, had disgusted him when he found them in Nance and Tisdale's files in Cape Girardeau, Missouri. He said he realized all the lies that had been told in the trial in front of the jury and to the judge himself were staggering. Phillip told the judge he had felt ashamed being an attorney because the system that had become so corrupt the pursuit of the truth was abandoned in this case. The judge let Phillip finish. Then he looked at the AUSA and asked him if he had anything to say. Descusio stood up and shrugged his shoulders and said, "Well, Your Honor, you know they didn't make those deals with me."

It looked like Judge Burns might explode. He seemed ready to come right out of his seat. As his face reddened, he said, "Mr. Descusio, you know that's no excuse. You know if these two men had a deal with the government anywhere in the world, it would be binding here."

Descusio said, "Yes. . . yes . . . Your Honor, but . . . but . . . I want it in the record that I-I-I didn't make those deals with those two men."

Phillip Watson stood up at that moment.

Mr. Watson: (Passing out more documents to the AUSA and the clerk who forwarded a copy to the judge.) Your Honor, I would like to enter these two letters into evidence as exhibits C and D.

Judge Burns: Very well (and the judge took a moment and read the short letters).

Mr. Watson: Judge Burns, as you can see, Your Honor, both of these letters are identical in content. They were both written by Hal Prince, AUSA for the Southeast District of Missouri. The letters are addressed to Mr. Nance's attorney in New Madrid, Missouri, and Mr. Tisdale's attorney in Sikeston, Missouri. I would further note the bottom paragraph of page one that continues over to page two. Just paraphrasing, Your Honor, but Mr. Prince says he has spoken to Terry Descusio, Assistant United States Attorney in Memphis, who assures their client of a deal to testify against Jack Phillips. Clearly, Your Honor, Mr. Prince meant Jack Phillips. Mr. Descusio had offered both Nance and Tisdale a deal to testify against Jack Phillips (and Kara Phillips, as it turned out). Please also note the date on the letters, Your Honor, May 19, 1998. These offers were made three months prior to the Phillips' trial. It's clear, Your Honor, their immunity and subsequent sentence reductions under Rule 35b stemmed directly from Mr. Descusio's offer of a deal. Mr. Descusio *did* have a deal with these witnesses. Your Honor, Mr. Descusio intentionally lied to you.

Judge Burns: Mr. Descusio?

Mr. Descusio: Well, Your Honor, you know I didn't write those letters to those attorneys.

Judge Burns: (Holding the letter in front of him.) I know you didn't write it, Mr. Descusio, but if you bring this letter into my courtroom, you made a deal! Just shut up and sit down.

The judge leaned back in his chair and appeared to be reading one of the letters again. He said to Phillip, "'Mr. Watson, would you like to call your next witness or adjourn for lunch? In fact, if you don't mind, Mr. Watson, I'd like to adjourn for lunch until 1:00 p.m. I have some matters in another case I need to deal with."

Mr. Watson: That's fine, Your Honor.

- The court was adjourned at 10:41 a.m. Phil had that twinkle in his eye that I had seen before when things went well on the football field. I was really excited. In just couple of hours, we had proventhat both Nance and Tisdale had multiple arrests previously and had lied about it,
- that Terry Descusio, the AUSA, had offered the witnesses a deal and let the witnesses perjure themselves and lie about it,
- that Terry Descusio, the AUSA, had lied about the deals himself to the jury and to the judge.

We hadn't brought up the affidavits and other things we had already for the hearing. The morning had gone great. I enjoyed our lunch that day even though it was in a holding cell. As I left the courtroom that morning, I saw the look on Paul's and Jen's and Brother John's faces. They looked so relieved! I wasn't sure what was coming, but we had won every claim, and Judge Burns knew it!

Chapter 22

Evidentiary Hearing, Afternoon, July 26, 1999

I was wondering if we were ever going to be able to bring up the fingerprints (or lack of fingerprints) in our case. The day of the fire, I had been threatened repeatedly that the authorities would take fingerprints, especially of the tools in the drawer of the metal desk that was found upstairs. The tools the authorities continually told me that "had not been damaged or affected by either the fire or the enormous amounts of water that was sprayed on the fire but never touched the tools." At trial, when we brought up the issue, the government denied any fingerprints had been taken. We knew better than that. Taking fingerprints from a crime scene was routine. We suspected the fingerprints only implicated Nance and Tisdale so rather than reporting that (as they were required by law to do since that evidence would have favored us) they just had that evidence disappear. I hoped we could get it in that day, but we didn't.

Judge Burns called the court into session that afternoon at 1:12 p.m. He looked at Phillip and said, "Call your next witness, Mr. Watson." Phillip began calling the men from Mason one by one to verify and testify to what they had sworn to in their affidavits. Descusio attempted to shake our first witness on cross-examination. However, he stuck to his guns and repeated over and over how he had personally heard Nance bragging about "getting off" by telling the authorities a teacher and his wife had a part in it.

After roughly nine men had testified, Mr. Descusio quit cross-examining witnesses and just sat at his table with his head in his hands looking down at the table. We could now add the following to our accomplishments that day:

- Keith's testimony from sentencing had been repeated and verified by the nine men that testified that day.
- Nance and Tisdale had both done a lot of talking and bragging at Mason in the dorms and on the rec yard.
- The previous evidence from that morning and the hour and a half of testimony that afternoon just confirmed that they were liars and totally unreliable as witnesses in regard to our case.

I thought Phillip had done a magnificent job of laying everything out in an orderly manner for the court. He had proven every accusation we had made in our motion. I had never felt better about our chances since the first day of the trial. While we were at lunch, Jen had called a really nice steak house and made reservations for us all to eat dinner. She even made a reservation for Kara, whom we thought could be home by that evening. She and Paul then convinced the judge would throw everything out just on the morning's testimony.

Judge Burns now asked Phillip, "Do you have any other witnesses, Mr. Watson?"

Phillip replied, "Just one more, Your Honor. I would like to call Mike Fields."

As we waited for the bailiff to bring him in, I asked Phillip, "What's he going to say?" Phillip told me he had gone to Mason the day before and interviewed Mike Fields. He didn't have time to tell me much more. All he said was, "Watch this, Coach. You are going to like this."

Mike Fields was sworn in. Phillip had him explain where he was housed in the Bureau of Prisons. He made sure the judge understood Fields was not in prison for anything related to our case or to the Nance/Tisdale case in Missouri. The questioning went like this:

Mr. Watson: Mr. Fields, let me ask you a question. Have you ever cooked meth before?

Mr. Fields: Yes.

Mr. Watson: Have you ever cooked meth with Mr. Nance and Tisdale?

Mr. Fields: Yes.

Mr. Watson: Tell us about it, please.

Mr. Fields: I sold meth for Nance and Tisdale in 1992 and 1993. In 1994 and 1995, I began cooking meth with them.

Mr. Watson: What was your role, and how many times did you cook meth with them?

Mr. Fields: I probably cooked meth with them twenty or thirty times. I did a little bit of everything: bought supplies, cooked flea powder, actually cooked the dope off, and I even made a booth to use to cook the meth more efficiently.

Mr. Watson: What happened to your booth?

Mr. Fields: It burned up in the fire in Memphis.

Mr. Watson: Mr. Fields, did you ever cook meth at 711 Highway 72 in Memphis?

Mr. Fields: Yes, I did.

Mr. Watson: When was that, Mr. Fields? Was it the day of the fire, that is July 13, 1997?

Mr. Fields: No, not July, not the day of the fire. I had cooked meth there before that, in May, on Memorial Day weekend, in 1997.

Mr. Watson: Mr. Fields, have you ever met Jack or Kara Phillips before seeing Mr. Phillips in court today?

Mr. Fields: No, sir.

Mr. Watson: So how did you happen to have cooked meth on their rented property in May of 1997?

Mr. Fields: I went down to Memphis with Timmy Tisdale.

Mr. Watson: Was Sam Nance with you?

Mr. Fields: No, sir. He was in his own car traveling about an hour behind coming from Missouri.

Mr. Watson: What was the date?

Mr. Fields: The last weekend in May, Memorial Day weekend, in 1997.

Mr. Watson: So you weren't there July 13, 1997, the day of the fire?

Mr. Fields: That's right. I was only there once, and that was in May. I wasn't there the day they had the fire.

Mr. Watson: Were Kara and Jack Phillips there when you cooked meth on the Memorial Day weekend in May of 1997?

Mr. Fields: No, they weren't there when we cooked meth in May.

Mr. Watson: Do you know where they were?

Mr. Fields: Timmy said they were out of town at some athletic event.

Mr. Watson: Will you tell us in your own words what happened that day when you cooked meth at 711 Highway 72?

Mr. Fields: Sure. Well, Timmy told me when we left Missouri that they would be gone out of town to an athletic event. We left Missouri and came up the Tennessee side. We left about 9:00 a.m., but when we drove by their house, their car was still there.

Mr. Watson: Do you know what time it was when you went by there?

Mr. Fields: It was about twelve o'clock, you know, lunchtime.

Mr. Watson: Okay, what happened next?

Mr. Fields: When we saw they was still home, I used Timmy's cell phone and called Sam, Sam Nance, and told him they was still home. We decided that me and Timmy would drive on down to the casinos in Tunica for a while. Sam said he would go by and check to see if they was still there when he got to Memphis in about an hour.

Mr. Watson: Okay, then what happened?

Mr. Fields: Me and Timmy went on down to Tunica. We had just got there when Sam called and said he was sitting down the street from their house in a bank parking lot and that he would watch the Phillips' house to see when they left.

Mr. Watson: The closest bank to the house is the bank at the comer of Kelly Price Road. How could Sam Nance see their house from there?

Mr. Fields: He had field binoculars. He said he would watch the house with his binoculars. Sam always kept binoculars in his glove box.

Mr. Watson: Is that all?

Mr. Fields: No. He called us back about twenty minutes later and said they was packing their car. While Timmy was talking to him, he told Timmy they was driving away. He told us to come on back to Memphis, and he said he would go ahead and get things started in the barn.

Mr. Watson: Did you and Tisdale return to Memphis?

Mr. Fields: Yeah, we left right then.

Mr. Watson: When you got back, did you, Tisdale, and Nance actually cook meth?

Mr. Fields: Yes.

Mr. Watson: How much meth did you and Nance and Tisdale cook that night?

Mr. Fields: We cooked between six and eight ounces.

Mr. Watson: If someone claimed they cooked a pound or even two pounds, would that be accurate?

Mr. Fields: No, it was between six and eight ounces.

Mr. Watson: How can you be so sure?

Mr. Fields: That's all we ever cooked. That's all we was set up to cook. We just set up and cooked overnight and then left wherever we was cooking. We only got supplies enough to cook six or eight ounces. We didn't have enough equipment or supplies to cook pounds.

Mr. Watson: What happened to the meth you cooked?

Mr. Fields: I took three ounces back to Missouri with me and sold two and did one myself. Nance and Tisdale split the rest.

Mr. Watson: Well, what did the Phillips get?

Mr. Fields: They didn't get nothing. They didn't know what was going on.

Judge Burns: Let me interrupt here for a moment, Mr. Fields. Do you have legal counsel here with you today?

Mr. Fields: No, Your Honor, I don't.

Judge Burns: Well, Mr. Fields, you do know you don't have any immunity here. You do know that you could be prosecuted. You have just admitted cooking meth and possessing with the intent to sale and deliver across state lines. You could get the same sentence Mr. Phillips received?

Mr. Fields: Yes, sir, I understand.

Mr. Watson: Your Honor, if I may, I think I can relieve your concern if I may?

Judge Burns: Go ahead, Mr. Watson.

Mr. Watson: (Turning to the witness, Mr. Fields.) Are you worried about telling the truth about you part in the manufacturing activities you took part in May 1997?

Mr. Fields: No, sir.

Mr. Watson: Would you tell us why you are not worried?

Mr. Fields: Yes, sir. I am not worried because I told all of this before.

Mr. Watson: To whom and when did you tell it, Mr. Fields?

Mr. Fields: I told it to an AUSA from Memphis in March of 1998.

Mr. Watson: Who was the Assistant United States Attorney from Memphis that you talked to?

Mr. Fields: It was an Assistant United States Attorney from Memphis with an Italian name.

(Everyone in the courtroom immediately turned and looked at AUSA Terry Descusio.)

Mr. Descusio: (Quickly rising.) It wasn't me, Your Honor!

Judge Burns motioned him to sit down.

Mr. Watson: Was it Mr. Descusio, Mr. Fields?

Mr. Fields: No, sir. It wasn't him.

Mr. Watson: Okay, Mr. Fields. So when did you talk to this AUSA?

Mr. Fields: It was in March 1998. He came to Marion (federal prison in Marion, Illinois) and interviewed me.

Mr. Watson: Did this Assistant United States Attorney record his interview with you?

Mr. Fields: I guess so. He laid down a tape recorder on the table and turned it on.

Mr. Watson: What did you tell him?

Mr. Fields: Just what I said today.

Mr. Watson: Is that why you're not worried about prosecution today because you already told this and didn't get prosecuted?

Mr. Fields: Yes.

Mr. Watson: Did this Assistant United States Attorney ask you if you knew Jack and/or Kara Phillips?

Mr. Fields: Yes, sir, he did.

Mr. Watson: And what did you say?

Mr. Fields: I said just what I said today. I ain't never met either one of them before. Your Honor, can I say something to Mr. Phillips?

Judge Burns: What did you want to say to Mr. Phillips?

Mr. Fields: I just wanted to tell him I'm sorry about him and his wife. I understand they both got a lot of time. I just wanted to apologize for being on that property and getting him and his wife in all this trouble.

Judge Burns: I think you just did apologize, Mr. Fields. Go ahead, Mr. Watson.

Mr. Watson: Let me ask you again, Mr. Fields, how much meth did you cook? I know you said six to eight ounces. If Sam Nance said you cooked two pounds, would that be the truth?

Mr. Fields: Sam would be wrong. We cooked between six and eight ounces, just like we always did.

Mr. Watson: Tell me again what happened to the dope.

Mr. Fields: I took three ounces back to Missouri. I did one myself and sold the owner two ounces. Sam and Timmy split what was left.

Mr. Watson: So what did the Phillips get?

Mr. Fields: Nothing. I told you the Phillips didn't know anything about what we was doing.

Mr. Watson: Thank you, Mr. Fields. No more questions, Your Honor.

Mr. Fields: (Looking up to the judge.) Judge Burns, can I ask you something?

Judge Burns: Sure, go ahead.

Mr. Fields: I've been held in the holding cell on his (pointing to Mr. Phillips) side where his people are being held. Should I be there or on the other side where Sam and Timmy are?

Judge Burns: Have you been threatened, Mr. Fields, or do you feel threatened on the Phillips' side?

Mr. Fields: No, sir.

Judge Burns: Then I think you should stay right where you are. You have really helped Mr. Phillips here today with your testimony. Mr. Watson, call your next witness.

Mr. Watson: I have no additional witnesses, Your Honor.

Judge Burns: Very well. Mr. Descusio, do you have any witnesses? Or do you wish to cross-examine?

Mr. Descusio: No, I do not wish to cross-examine, and I have no witnesses to offer, Your Honor.

Judge Burns: Very well. Then let's hear your closing statements. Mr. Watson.

Mr. Watson: Your Honor, my client and his wife were denied due process of law in not being properly informed about the deals the witnesses against them had with the government. We acknowledge there was some circumstantial evidence against the defendants. However, they would not have been convicted without the testimony of Sam Nance and Timmy Tisdale. Not only were the deals withheld, but their arrests were also concealed in regard to the credibility of the witnesses. The deals and arrests were withheld from you too, Your Honor, and from the jury. The Assistant United States Attorney knew the truth about the deals and the arrests. He allowed the perjured testimony, and there is an alarming amount of evidence that he might have even orchestrated it. As an officer of the court, he fouled our system. He perverted justice. That resulted in ruining the lives of two innocent people and of falsely convicting them of a crime he should have known that they didn't commit.

That's not all. The United States Attorneys Office here in Memphis withheld exculpatory evidence. The taped statement from Mr. Fields that completely exonerated both Jack and Kara Phillips was withheld and should have been turned over to the defense prior to trial. We still have not received either the tape or a transcript from that interview with Mr. Fields. The United States Attorneys Office cannot deny this. They added Mr. Fields to their witness list. They transported him from Marion, Illinois, to Mason, Tennessee, for the Phillips' trial. Your Honor, they knew they were not going to call Mr. Fields. He would have blown their theory of the case right out of the water. In a real sense, they defrauded the citizens of this country by wasting taxpayer money to transport and house Mr. Fields even though they knew they were not going to call him. The only possible explanation is they put him on their witness list to protect him and hide him from the defense in case the defense somehow found out about him. Mr. Descusio allowed Mr. Nance and Mr. Tisdale to testify that they alone cooked meth there in May of 1997 knowing that Mr. Fields was there with them.

In fact, the only way the government could have even found out about Mr. Fields would have been from Nance and Tisdale. We can assume that since they had already told the government about Fields, the only way they would omit him from their trial testimony is if they had been instructed to do so by the prosecution. The fact Mr. Descusio did nothing to correct this incorrect testimony seems to indicate he is the person responsible for orchestrating perjured testimony. Added with the lying by the witnesses regarding their arrest records and the testimony by the inmates to whom they bragged about playing the game in the system to avoid prosecution, my client demands justice. It is clear the Phillips suffered an injustice in this case and continues to do so every day they remain incarcerated. Thank you, Your Honor.

Judge Burns: Thank you, Mr. Watson. Mr. Descusio, can we hear from you?

Mr. Descusio: Your Honor . . . I only . . . there's just one . . . the only thing is Jack and Kara Phillips had a fair trial and were found guilty. Now counsel, counsel comes in . . . and he, he calls me a liar and suggests we messed up this case. I would . . . could remind you, judge of all the evidence of the defendants buying supplies and being involved. Your Honor, they lived there where they were cooking meth at that house. The government resents the accusations made by counsel.

Judge Burns: Thank you, gentlemen. I will review the record here and render my decision in short order. This court is adjourned.

It was 4:30 p.m. What a wonderful, beautiful day! Paul and Jen were excited. We wouldn't get to keep that reservation today, but it sure looked like we would really soon. I was excited too. I hugged

Phillip and told him that I loved him and he had done a magnificent job. Paul and Jen were hugging on him too. Descusio and March just scuttled out the door without looking at anyone or anything. They didn't say a word to anyone. I was sure wishing Kara was there to share this special moment. I knew I would see her soon. My thought was that we would be home for Thanksgiving and Christmas after missing both those holidays the year before.

Paul said he would tell Mom and Dad how well everything had gone. Mary Lynn and Carey would be excited too. All the hard work we had done—Paul, Phillip, me, and even Keith—had paid off for us. Phillip said he would be out to see me soon and for me to call him tomorrow.

I was taken into custody by the Marshals and escorted out then handcuffed and returned to the holding cell. By 6:30 p.m., I was back at FCI Memphis. I told Keith all that had happened after he had testified. We prepared a celebratory meal fit for a king. Finally, I felt like that old door was starting to crack open. Word spread around the unit and compound, and many other inmates came by to congratulate me on our success in court that day. I wrote Kara a long detailed letter and let her know I would see her soon! The nightmare was almost over!

Chapter 23

Back at FCI Memphis

As the softball season ended and the summer faded into the fall, everyone in the Phillips clan was exhilarated with the possibilities. Our optimism was almost visible. It was as if we were all on an adrenaline rush. We were waiting for news any day that our situation had been reversed. I was planning on petitioning to get my teaching job back.

Football season began that fall. In August, when all the high school teams started practicing, I began to miss coaching. I hadn't coached a game in eight years, but it was in my blood. I guess my problem was that I began to doubt that I would ever be allowed to coach again. Even if my conviction was overturned, would anyone want a high school coach who had gotten all the bad publicity I had received to coach their kids? I doubted it.

The same thing began to creep in my head regarding my teaching. I was a great teacher, and I knew it. I felt like I could never teach again in Memphis or Shelby County considering what had happened and all publicity associated with Kara and me. I tried to keep my hopes alive regarding the teaching (and coaching). However, as the days, weeks, and months passed, and I didn't receive one letter, not one letter, from any of my teaching colleagues or administrators, I knew I was out and would never be allowed to teach in the Mid-South again. It broke my heart. It tempered my enthusiasm about getting out.

When the college and pro football seasons started in September, the *Commercial Appeal*, the Memphis newspaper, ran a contest in the paper called the "Dandy Dozen." They listed twelve of the top college games coming up that next week and encouraged their readers to pick the winners. One also had to pick the number of points that would be scored in one of the games in case there was a tie for winning teams, which would serve as the tiebreaker. The weekly winners would go into a pool, and at the end of the season, the paper would draw one name from all the winners to win five hundred dollars.

To play each week, I had to call an 800 number. I would be asked to enter my social security number then choose my teams. I had played the contest before I was incarcerated. It was fun and interesting. My situation was that I couldn't actually play the contest because we were not allowed to call any 800 number. My brother, Paul, played the contest each week. We decided we would just compete with each other and see who could pick the most correct games. I had a subscription for the paper that Jen paid for each year. Each week I would pour over the twelve games and make my picks. When I called Paul on Thursday nights, we would go through the games. He would tell me who he picked and I would tell him who I picked. Whoever won bragged and rubbed it in when the games were over. The loser just made excuses why he and his chosen teams had lost. It was really great fun for two brothers and two old coaches. We had played about six weeks when an incident associated with the contest occurred.

One afternoon I was at work at food service when a call came over the intercom for Jack Phillips to report to the lieutenant's office. I dropped what I was doing, walked over to the lieutenant's office, and knocked on the door and waited to be invited in. Eventually, I heard someone say, "Come in."

I went in and a lieutenant was standing behind the desk. He asked to see my ID, so I gave it to him. He then said to me, "Phillips, you've been given a shot." A shot was a disciplinary write-up. It could mean a slap on the wrist for doing something wrong, extra duty, a trip to the Shu, and/or even losing good-time credit depending on the seriousness of the infraction. I couldn't imagine what I had done to be given a disciplinary shot.

I asked the lieutenant, "Sir, could you tell me why I've been given a shot? What have I done wrong?"

He said, "This shot is for gambling on the telephone."

I said, "Sir, I don't gamble. And if I did, I wouldn't do it on the telephone knowing you listen and record our phone calls. How was I gambling and with whom?" I assumed they just had the wrong person.

He replied, "Didn't you just discuss with your brother [he gave me his phone number] twelve football games and pick the winners and point spreads? Let's see, that was Thursday night."

I was shocked. I began to try to explain to the lieutenant that we were just picking some games from the paper's football contest. I told him I couldn't play the contest really because I couldn't call the 800 number I had to call to play. I also explained that couldn't be gambling because gambling was illegal in Tennessee and the paper couldn't be running a gambling game every week in the paper. I told him my brother and I were old football coaches and we were just picking the games against each other for fun and something to do. I even told him I had saved the "Dandy Dozen" game for that week and could bring it to him and show it to him.

All he said was, "You'll have a disciplinary hearing, and you can explain all that then." He handed me the paperwork and said, "Sign right there," indicating a line at the bottom of the shot. I signed the document and took my copy. I was extremely upset.

There were full-fledged gambling tickets each week on the compound. Those gambling tickets took in thousands of dollars in stamps each week. Often the bookies couldn't pay their debts and had to check into protective custody. There were men who were beaten up over gambling debts and men who were making weekly or monthly payments trying to catch up on an old debt. Losers often had to have their families send them money to pay gambling debts. Even though I wasn't involved, ever, in any of that, I had been given a shot for gambling! It didn't make sense. Was I being paranoid? I began to think that too.

There was an older black inmate who had been a minister in East St. Louis, Illinois. He also owned a car lot and was extremely active in the church and religious community in and around St. Louis. He often preached in the prison church and helped the chaplains in myriad of ways. He had a reputation in the prison among the inmates as a snitch because he was too close and too friendly with the stuff and guards. When I told him about the shot, he said, "Give it to me, Jack. I'll go to the captain and take care of this."

I had run off several copies of the shot. I took one to my counselor, Mr. Wren. He coached peewee football in Memphis and had for many years. He loved athletics. I showed him the hot and the "Dandy Dozen" contest where I had marked the teams and explained how my brother and I played it against one another every week. I also pointed out it was illegal to gamble in Tennessee, so that contest was not gambling.

He said, "Hell, I play that game every week myself! That's not gambling. What are they trying to do? Don't worry about it, Phillips. I'll take care of this."

I don't know if it was the preacher or the counselor, but I was told to tear up the shot, that it had been withdrawn. I was grateful to my friend and to Mr. Wren for being willing to help me. I'm not fully convinced the staff would have ever believed just me. I could have been put in the hole for sixty days while they investigated the matter.

Chapter 24

Mental Illness

All of us inmates were worried about our mental health. It was a strain mentally on every inmate, especially those with long sentences. Mental illness was real at FCI Memphis. It wasn't restricted to any age group, race, or nationality. It was an ever-present reality we all lived with. It wasn't quite an insane asylum, but it wasn't very far removed from that.

One of the most bizarre mentally ill men was a small black man in his late twenties. He was on some heavy medication. I am not sure what he was taking, but we could all tell when he wasn't taking it. On his meds, he smiled a lot and was well-groomed. His clothes were always starched and pressed, his boot shined, and the top button of his shirt was buttoned securely around his neck. In retrospect, I guess he wasn't much different than the one hundred or so men that lined up for pill line every day at 6:00 a.m., 3:00 p.m., and 8:00 p.m.

One day in August of 1999, while we were all walking up to chow and lining up outside to go in and be served, the young black man bolted and ran full speed toward the front gate. It was a thick heavy metal gate set into a brick archway, the primary entrance onto the compound. Beyond the gate was about forty feet of open space and then a door into the control center. It was impossible to get out of the institution that way.

This young man charged the initial gate set into the brick archway and climbed the fence about halfway up and began rocking and attempting to shake the secure heavy gate and screaming, "Let my people go! Let my people go!" He screamed over and over and over again. I had never seen such bizarre behavior. Everyone on the compound just stopped and watched what was happening. The officers didn't get too excited. They stood around and watched a while themselves. The officers slowly grouped up and headed over and peeled him off the gate. Although the man was small, it took at least ten officers to pry him loose. The inmate was sent off somewhere to a mental facility, but he returned about six weeks later back on his meds. He again appeared rather docile and smiled and dressed immaculately.

It didn't last long. Within two weeks, there was another episode. I walked into our unit (Beale-B) one day while everyone else was at lunch. The dayroom was absolutely empty. The only other person I saw in the unit was this same young black man. He was still dressed in his pressed uniform with his top button on his shirt buttoned. He was standing on the landing on the stairs near my cell. His feet were about even with the top of my head as he stood on the landing about halfway up. When I walked in, I saw him standing there with both hands tightly grasping the railing around the landing. He was rocking back and forth and emitting a strange noise, a noise somewhere between moaning and grunting. The sound was unearthly.

As I approached the landing cautiously (I had to go right by it to get to my cell), I looked up at his face. His eyes were rolled up in the back of his head. All I could see was the white in his eyes. That vision, along with the horrendous sounds coming out of him, made every hair on my body stand up and gave me a chill right down to my bones. He was mentally in a place I had never been and certainly never wanted to go.

I began looking around the unit for someone. I looked in the unit officer's office, but no one was there. There was not another inmate in the entire unit. Just as I had decided to leave the unit and get someone, the officer came from the middle hallway that connected Beale-A and Beale-B. I shouted at him when he saw me, "Hey, Officer, you better come see this!"

He came across the dayroom and said, "What is it, Phillips?"

I just looked up and said, "Look at him, Officer."

He looked up at the man for a moment and said, "Oh my god! What's wrong with him?" I told him I didn't know, but he had better get some help because that inmate was obviously out of his mind again. Eventually several officers showed up. They took custody of the man, and I never saw him again.

Another mentally ill man in our unit was a big Cuban we all called Junior. One of his legs was extremely misshapened, and he was crippled. As a result, he had a hard time sitting. He spent most of his time in a kneeling position on both knees. In fourteen months, I never saw him ever sit in a chair. Even in food service, he got on his knees and ate off his tray on the table. He was tall enough to do that. The officers knew him, and he had obviously been there a while. They hardly noticed his odd behavior.

He also watched TV sitting on his knees. He had a difficult time of realizing that what he was watching on TV was not real, not reality. In a Western action movie, he would sit totally engrossed in the action. When someone got shot or blown up or died on TV, Junior would lie in the floor and weep like a baby. He must have been forty years old, but we could not explain to him that what he had seen on TV was not real—that the actor had not really been shot and wasn't really dead. He took it personally and grieved and literally sobbed.

Junior was really softhearted. We had a flock of a dozen or so ducks that stayed in a nearby pond. They knew when it was feeding time at the prison. They always flew in and lined the sidewalk coming out of the cafeteria. The officers often had to stand over Junior and make him eat or he would take all his food outside and feed the ducks. He would feed them every bite of his own food.

At one point, I don't know if he was missing his meds or what, but he sat in his cell for thirty-nine days and did not come out. I would walk by his cell and look in through the glass on his door, and he would be sitting naked on his bunk masturbating. That was the only thing he did. His weight tumbled from about 220 pounds to around 150 pounds. He had no food in his cell. He did have water, and I guess he drank some or he would have died, but he never ate and wouldn't come out. They finally went in and got him and shipped him off for psychiatric care someplace. He had been at that facility for almost 20 years. Each time they had to send him off, he would be gone for 6–8 months. No one could tell us how many times he had been sent off and returned. He no doubt was mentally ill.

There were a few other inmates that suffered from obvious mental illnesses. They caught two of the Mexican cooks mixing our meatloaf in a sink. They had thoroughly scrubbed and cleaned the sink. They had used it many times to mix meatloaf. This particular time, they were caught mixing in real human feces. The officers had to put them in protective custody or the other inmates would have killed them. They had been cooks there for many years. No one knew if they had done this before, but everyone assumed they had.

There were two middle-aged white men that mixed up the Kool-Aid and tea for the inmates in the Shu. They put the drinks in large orange containers with spouts. The men in Shu were given Styrofoam cups with their choice of drink with every meal. These two men had held the job of preparing those drinks for fourteen years. Early one morning, an officer walked into their work area and observed both of them urinating into those containers. No one could determine how long they had been doing that either.

Mental illness there was not just confined to the inmates. There were officers suffering all types of mental illness as well because their job was stressful and depressing. I wasn't surprised to find many of the officers suffered psychological problems. The black cook-foreman that had been so evil to me, Mr. House, had his issues. After I became clerk and no longer worked for him, he showed up at my office work area early one morning and wanted to talk. He went to both ends of the L-shaped hallway and locked the heavy doors so we wouldn't be interrupted. He confided to me that he had sat on his stairway at his home the night before with a .357 Magnum pistol contemplating blowing his brains out. In fact, he said the only reason he hadn't was because his five-year-old daughter came up the stairs, put her arms around his neck as he hid the gun below his legs on the stairs, and said, "Daddy, don't be so sad. Don't you know I love you?" As he told me, a flood of tears streamed down his face. He said if she had not come up those stairs just when she did, he would be dead. He was absolutely sure he would have killed himself.

All of Mr. House's problems were job related. He had abandoned his own dreams for the security of a good, regular paycheck. He spent the next three weeks with me about three hours a day. We read a lot of scripture, and I listened to him a lot. He wanted to own and operate his own restaurant. He even picked out a location and was trying to get financing to fulfill his dream to be his own boss in his own restaurant. He eventually quit the Bureau of Prisons and did just that.

An assistant food service administrator transferred into Memphis in the fall of 1999 from California. In his midthirties, he had been Federal Bureau of Prisons Employee of the Year in 1998. He was a real hotshot and gung ho, even coming to work on his days off. From the director to the lowest inmate, including me, he had made everyone miserable. He was devious and wicked, making up false accusations about other staff members and lying about the inmates. At one point, he didn't show up to work for three weeks. No one could reach him, so they finally sent someone check on him at home. His wife and children had left him a month before and returned to California. When they entered his house, they found him hanging from a banister with a rope around his neck. He had left a suicide note on the floor right below him surrounded by his bills and a nasty note to his wife.

These are just some examples of the mental illness we lived with at that facility. My best guess would be that 25 percent to 35 percent of the population was severely mentally ill and another 40 percent had mild mental illnesses. Men and women just can't cope in an environment like a prison. We are social creatures, and you can't deprive a man or woman of social stimuli and not see it result in mental illness. The entire environment is so surreal. We all worried about it as we struggled to remain mentally healthy.

I know Morgan Green, the lifetime inmate who befriended me, once asked me, "Jack, how much time you got?" I told him my sentence was 262 months. He did the calculation in his head. He then asked me how I was doing, and I told him, "Fine, I guess." I'll never forget what he told me that day. He said, "Listen, I want to tell you something. After you've done about ten or eleven years, you'll know if you' re going to make it or not. If you're not nuts by then, you'll probably be okay. It takes about that long to wear on a man. If you're still sane after ten or eleven years, you'll probably be all right. If not, you'll be more like Junior or one of these other nuts. By the way, you will be the last one to know you are nuts."

I continued to constantly examine myself to test my mental health. I grew distrustful of my own evaluation. I fought depression and loneliness every day, I know that. The nights were the worst. Going to bed meant real stress in regard to loneliness for me. It was my constant companion. It was difficult having my wife's loving arms around me or not being able to hold my wife's hand. The mental illness reality seemed more threatening than the possibility of physical violence.

Chapter 25

Hope Is a Fragile Thing

As September turned to October, we were still soaring on the wings of optimism from our evidentiary hearing back in July. Our release still seemed imminent. I found myself replaying how it might happen beginning with a call over the intercom for inmate Phillips to report to R and D. How exciting! Every time there was an announcement, I half-expected to hear that message.

On October 1, 1999, Keith Hawkins and I were sitting in the dayroom watching the 6:00 p.m. local news on Channel 3 in Memphis. I don't recall anything about that newscast except the very last story. The anchorwoman said that Federal Judge Jason T. Burns had temporarily left the bench due to a medical condition. She went on to explain he had suffered a recurrence of a cancer condition. He had battled cancer a few years before, she said, and it had been in remission. I was stunned. Of course, I wondered how this might affect the decision on the events of the evidentiary hearing.

I called Paul that night, and he had seen the same news report. He assured me he would start trying to call Phillip Watson immediately. He wanted to find out how this would affect the decision we were waiting for from our hearing. Don't misunderstand, we were still totally confident of the outcome. Kara and I had both written each other that we hoped to be home by Thanksgiving this year and certainly no later than Christmas. Now, with Judge Burns not at work, that looked more improbable but certainly not impossible.

The *Commercial Appeal* carried the same news in an article about the judge's condition the next day. I called Paul after day two of the news, and he said he had talked to Phillip, and Phillip didn't think it would affect us one way or the other. That was so encouraging. He said about the only thing was that the decision could possibly be delayed by the judge's illness. He wanted Paul to assure Kara and me that nothing substantial had changed. However, I had that same old nagging feeling that I had the day of the fire when I saw all the law enforcement people in plain clothes milling about the property. I just wasn't comfortable with the new developments.

October turned into November, and Thanksgiving came and went. We had a good meal at the institution, but the family struggled again because of our absence. I wondered if they would ever have a normal holiday while we were gone.

Kara was becoming more restless too. She was so homesick and beginning to feel forgotten. She had only two visits since she had gone to Fort Worth ten months before. Paul, Mary Lynn, and the grandchildren began planning a visit to Fort Worth near Christmas. The thought of a Christmas visit seemed to cheer her up a little bit. She was still feeling isolated and lonely, and because she was so far away from the family, she felt completely cutoff. I hurt for her, but while I was struggling with my own problems, her problems bothered me more than my own. We had now been incarcerated for a year and a half. If this is what I was going to have to deal with for the next eighteen years, I had to ask myself if it was really worth it. I felt like the time was doing me, not me doing the time. There is a big difference in prison, and I was only at the beginning of this dark journey. So was Kara.

Chapter 26

FCI Memphis and the Church

I don't think I could have made it through those holiday seasons and that first year had it not been for the church. The chaplain there was an older black man. He was a nervous Nellie type person, but he knew the Bible, was doctrinally sound, and loved the Lord. I really appreciated his preaching. He also allowed a few inmates who were ordained ministers on the outside to preach (yes, I met many, many ordained ministers in prison). We had a great choir. It was made up of a diverse group of men that sang as if they were singing to the Lord.

Because we were in the city of Memphis, we had access to many wonderful volunteer groups that visited the prison on a regular basis. The prison ministry was outstanding. My favorite volunteer was Ms. Peggy Goodlett. Her husband was on death row in a Mississippi state prison, and her son was serving a life sentence in the same prison. She understood us and our needs. She brought joy to the compound every Wednesday night when she came for Bible study. Her topics for Bible study were interesting and relevant. She had her finger on the pulse of our spiritual needs, and she understood exactly where we were mentally, emotionally, and spiritually. She and I formed a warm bond that has lasted to this day.

Mrs. Goodlett brought a missionary friend of hers (every Wednesday night for a month). This younger black woman was full of energy and enthusiastic about her mission. I let her read a few articles I had written, and she got all excited and asked if she could take them with her. The next week she showed up with some contracts for me to sign that would allow a new Christian magazine to publish my articles. She asked, and I agreed to be a featured writer for this magazine. Its first issue was due to be released in just a few months. I signed the papers.

When Ms. Peggy showed up the next Wednesday night, I was already in the chapel waiting to talk to her missionary friend. I had forgotten the name of the new magazine and wanted to touch base on the exact date it was to be published and make sure I had a subscription. When Ms. Peggy came in, her friend wasn't with her. I asked, "Where's your friend, Ms. Peggy?"

She said, "Well, she's gone and won't be back for sometime. She was called and asked to do a mission trip to India, and she accepted." Ms. Peggy assured me she would try to get an address for me so I could contact her about the magazine. Ms. Peggy was excited about the project as well.

Sadly, I never made contact with the lady who had gone to India again. I never found out if the magazine came out, what the name of the magazine was, and if my articles were in it or not. Ms. Peggy continued to come faithfully on Wednesday night and occasionally brought other guests with her. She had a full-time job but still found time to come minister to a group of inmates. I know the Lord has special rewards for people like her and the volunteers that visit jails and prisons weekly with no earthly acclaim.

Brother John faithfully sent me all kinds of religious materials I requested, including copies or manuscripts of his new books. He continued a fast pace of publishing book after book. Paul, of course, was my chief supplier of both religious and secular books. My nightly Bible-study classes were enriching and helped us get through the holiday seasons and the tough days in the institution (and there were plenty of those days). We wrote down our prayer requests each night. It was amazing that very few requests involved the inmate that made the request. Most requests were about family members and problems they faced on the outside, for wives or mothers that were struggling to raise the children while the fathers were away. We also prayed for a change in the draconian laws that were handing down sentences that far exceeded the crime. When a holiday night came around, we would go back to the previous holiday and read all the prayer requests that had been made, noting how many had been answered. It often took us two nights to cover it all. The Lord miraculously heard and answered so many of our prayers! It was a comfort to know that He was hearing us and actually moving on our deepest needs in ways that could only be described as miraculous.

I continued to write Kara a letter every day. It was therapeutic for me, and I know it helped her. I wrote others faithfully as well. Sadly, my ninety-five-year-old grandmother passed away while I was at FCI Memphis. I had enjoyed writing to her and receiving her letters ever since the first week I was incarcerated. She was such a blessing to me. Because of her, I had read the Bible all the way through from front to back. I have read it twice more since then. She had written me early on that she had just finished reading it cover to cover for the fifteenth time when she was ninety-four. That motivated me to do it too. She was an outstanding Christian woman whose love for me never wavered.

Chapter 27

Christmas at FCI Memphis

Christmas rolled in, and we still hadn't heard a decision regarding our evidentiary hearing from July. As far as we knew, Judge Burns was still absent from the bench. This would be our second year to miss Christmas. It was not any easier for Kara and me the second time around.

Missing Christmas at Mason the first year was one thing. I was missing Christmas the second year in the Bureau of Prisons. In the BOP, we would have Christmas packages with all kinds of foods and snacks we couldn't buy at the commissary. Anything different means a lot in prison.

The BOP also had Christmas decoration competitions between the units and even the departments. Prizes were awarded to the winners, and photographs of the winning decorations would be taken and posted on bulletin boards all over the compound. The competitions were intense. Pizza dinners (from Pizza Hut) were at stake for the inmates. Staff members from the winning departments also received nice prizes.

The real surprise was how seriously the inmates took the Christmas decorating competition. Maybe because the average stay of an inmate at that institution seemed to be about twenty years, the inmates went all out in decorating. They could tell you stories about the winning decorations from years before. There were Santa sleighs and reindeers, holly everywhere, and manger scenes. Some of the decorations had been made and used in the past and stored somewhere for future use. Some of the decorations had been purchased by staff members. All the housing units were decorated inside and out. The decorations included lights and a Christmas tree all trimmed out in each unit and in virtually every department of the institution. It was Christmas everywhere in prison!

One man in our unit had been incarcerated in that same unit for twenty-five years. He had built a small wooden house. It was the size of a child's very large dollhouse. An inmate could stoop down and walk inside it. He had also built the house so the roof could be easily removed and the walls taken down in pieces. The house had three floors in it. He had even hand carved tiny pieces of furniture to fully decorate each room in the house. He had wired the house to be powered by four D batteries, so the house even had lights. When the dayroom was dark and the lights in the little house were on, it was quite beautiful. He had turned it into a gorgeous little Christmas house.

Officers and inmates alike came over to look at the Christmas house in our unit (they allowed the inmates to come in to take a look). This man had poured three years of his life into working on and finishing this magnificent piece of art. Everyone that saw it was amazed. Therefore, no one was surprised when Beale-B (my unit) won the prize for Christmas decorations with this house as the centerpiece. Not only did we get a pizza dinner, but our unit got to eat first in the chow hall for the next week. Inmates in our unit had worked so hard in stringing lights and holly and making the unit look as Christmasy as it could be, and it paid off.

The day after our unit won the competition, an inmate photographer came over to take photos of the winning decorations to be posted all over the compound. He came near mealtime. Keith and I were the only inmates in the unit when he came.

I don't think we actually said we had anything to do with the house or decorating the unit. I do believe the cameraman thought both of those things were true. He ended up asking Keith and me to pose with all the decorations and in all the photos he took of the prize winning decorations. We posed by the house, the Christmas tree, inside the unit, and outside the unit. He must have taken twenty or so pictures. When the photos were developed and posted, Keith and

I were in every picture. We received congratulations from many staff members and other inmates on the festive job we had done decorating Beale-B for Christmas.

Truthfully, we had not lifted one hand to do any decorating. We had not hung anything on the tree, hung a light, hung a piece of holly, and certainly not worked on the house. Keith and I laughed till we cried about the folly of it all. The other inmates in our unit didn't think it was so funny.

The family did make the trip to see Kara, and right after Christmas they all came to visit me, including Mom and Dad. Dad was in a wheelchair now, but it was still great to see them. It hurt to see them leave, and I know it was hard for them to leave me behind.

We all survived Y2K that year as well. The doomsayers were all saying everything (including every computer) would crash and things would be in turmoil. The staff had put up a memo that if there was any kind of computer crash, we would all be locked down until it was resolved. That meant locked in our cell twenty-four hours a day. There were no problems, so that lockdown was avoided.

We were routinely locked in our cells at count time at 4:00 p.m., 10:00 p.m., and 10:00 a.m. on weekends and holidays. The count only took five to ten minutes max, but they often kept us locked down forty-five minutes or even an hour just because they could. It made their jobs easier because they didn't have to deal with an inmate during those locked down count times. We were also locked down 10:30 p.m. each weeknight and 2:30 a.m. each weekend night. If there was a fight or other problem, we were put on twenty-four-hour lockdown. Once we were locked down for three straight weeks because of gang violence in the prison. Our meals were brought to our cell, and the trays were shoved though a slot that was made in the thick metal doors. Each third day of the lockdown staff came by and unlocked our door and gave us five minutes to take a shower and return. It was extremely boring, and it didn't take long to get somewhat claustrophobic. As a result, I always tried to keep a few books in my locker and plenty of snacks to tide me over in case of a lockdown. The really painful part was we were not allowed to use the phones, visitation was cancelled, and all our religious services were cancelled.

Chapter 28

February 12, 2000

February 12, 2000, was on a Saturday. It marked the second anniversary of our arrest which ultimately led to our conviction and incarceration. Following our arrest on February 12, 1998, we had spent five days locked up over a holiday weekend (President's Day) waiting for our bail to be posted. We had now been incarcerated about 18 months since our conviction.

I was in the dayroom watching TV at Beale-B when there was a news flash about 9:20 p.m. that broke up the regular programming. The breaking news was the Federal Judge Jason T. Burns, age fifty-six, had just passed away.

It was a shocking piece of news. I had just never considered that Judge Burns would actually die. I'll admit, one part of me wanted to celebrate. I had no love for Judge Burns for allowing our trial to proceed and end the way it did. The other part of me was upset and full of uncertainty. What about the evidentiary hearing? We had all been anxiously awaiting a decision (a positive decision, we believed) in regard to our hearing on July 26, 1999. I knew the judge had taken ill and left the bench on October 1, 1999. I thought he was taking a break to recover and did not expect it to end in his death. I had not considered that he might die without having ruled on our hearing. I couldn't help but wonder if he had ruled and we just hadn't heard his decision.

I jumped up and called Paul. He said he had just seen the report on another Memphis TV station. He assured me he would again call Phillip and find out what it all might mean to us. He reached Phillip on Sunday, February 13, and Phillip said he would check on things Monday morning when the courthouse opened. That was the best we could do.

We had been so hopeful and sure we would win the evidentiary hearing. Winning would mean the government would choose not to prosecute or try us again because Nance and Tisdale's testimony would be tainted to such a point that it would be ineffectual. Surely too the government knew we would call Mike Fields. His testimony would nullify anything Nance or Tisdale might say, and we could also call R. A. Boone. He would deny his involvement at all. Why wouldn't he? We didn't expect he would testify that he cooked meth there and risk going to jail himself.

After seven months of waiting for a decision, I will admit our confidence had wavered. Still, hope is the most powerful force an inmate has. We were still confident our time in prison was going to be short, maybe we would be home soon although we had missed our second Thanksgiving and our second Christmas. I guess we were more uncertain than doubtful. But the uncertainly had cut into our confidence. I didn't hold many good feelings about Judge Burns. I felt that he had sentenced us harshly and that he lacked the courage to overturn the verdict when he knew we were not guilty. He had all but admitted that at sentencing with his remarks. I felt it was cowardly for him to have not done the right thing; nevertheless, I didn't want him to die. He was familiar with the intricacies of the case, and he had heard all the evidence and seen the faces of those who had been caught with their pants down. That was priceless. The tone of the evidentiary hearing was just about as important as the content. Our judge had now gone to face the real judge.

When Paul reached Phillip on the phone Monday, Phillip said he hadn't been able to learn anything. He was convinced no decision had been made regarding our case or what should or should not happen as a result of Judge Burns's death. He told Paul to tell Kara and me to be as patient as possible. He assured Paul he would let him know the minute he learned anything.

Phillip called Paul with news on Tuesday morning. Phillip had just arrived at his office, and he had news. He had received a decision from the court on his fax machine regarding our evidentiary hearing. It had been sent from the clerk's office fax machine on Monday evening at 11:59 p.m.! Who was in the clerk's office at 11:59 p.m.? Phillip said it was a one-sentence denial of our motion to reconsider the preceding motion for a new trial that we had filed. Phillip said the sum was that our motion had "no merit."

It read, "Your motion for reconsideration of the motion that had been denied for a new trial is denied because your motion lacked merit."

Phillip faxed copies to Paul and mailed copies to both Kara and me. There were several real concerns about this document. First, it wasn't filed until Monday, February 14. According to the document, Judge Burns had signed it on February 4. (Remember, he had died on the 12.) If he signed it on the fourth of February, where had it been for ten days? Why had an entire week passed by without it being filed? Secondly, who filed it? Judge Turner obviously didn't. He wasn't around on Monday the fourteenth to file it? Thirdly, the denial was so sparse there wasn't really anything to appeal from the denial. It didn't address the deals, the arrests records, the letters, the lying, the affidavits, and the testimony of the witnesses. It just said it lacked merit. Well, we knew it had enough merit for the judge to grant an evidentiary hearing that probably cost the government at least one hundred thousand dollars!

Lester Moore had filed the first motion for retrial based on newly discovered evidence. His motion was only a page and a half long. Judge Burns had denied that motion. The judge's denial on that motion was a full two pages that addressed each issue. He had gone into great detail as to why each of Lester's points had been denied.

Phillip's motion to reconsider was twenty-seven pages long. We had been granted an evidentiary hearing that lasted an entire day. Nine witnesses had testified. This denial supposedly from Judge Burns didn't address any specific issue or testimony. It just said it "lacked merit." It did not go through each of our claims, point by point, explaining the denial. Judge Burns just did not do this type of sloppy work, yet the document bore his signature.

Furthermore, the denial wasn't filed until two days *after* the judge had died. I couldn't help but wonder, who stuck that document in that fax machine to Phillip's fax number at 11:59 p.m. in the courthouse? There really was no rush to get that decision to us that night. I finally received my copy of the denial from Phillip on Thursday, February 17.

The denial decision document looked even worse than it sounded and created all kinds of alarms in my mind. The most astounding thing was to just look at Judge Burns's signature. It just didn't look right. For one thing, it was about a quarter inch above the signature line. I had four or five documents of my own with Judge Burns's signature. His signature was buried on the line in all those signatures.

I took the documents to food service and used the copy machine to blow up those signatures until they would only fit on legal-sized paper (8 1/2 by 14). Keith and I took colored pencils and began to document the differences in the signatures. Together we found at least twenty-five abnormalities. I had gathered up documents signed by Judge Burns from other inmates. We had about twenty signature pages with Judge Burns's signature on them. Based on what we found, we believed the signature on the document in question was clearly fraudulent.

An inmate that lived in Delta Unit that Keith and I had both met and talked with was a professional forger who had made everything from bogus driver's licenses to phony passports. He said he had been a professional forger for over fifty years and had this one and only conviction on his record.

On Saturday, February 19, 2000 (Kara's forty-seventh birthday), we asked him if he would meet with us and take a look at some signatures for us. He agreed to do so. We had twenty-three documents to look at, counting our document. They were all blown up to the same size on legal paper on the same copy machine.

Keith and I met the man on what we called Mud Island at FCI Memphis. Mud Island consisted of several concrete picnic tables connected by sidewalks. The entire area near the sidewalks was covered in pea gravel. There were even a couple of trees that provided shade for the area. It sat right out in the middle of the compound and was a common gathering place for inmates during the warm weather months.

I told the man we suspected at least one of the signatures was bogus. We asked him to look at the signatures on the documents and see if he could reasonably determine if one was a forged or bogus signature. He said he would do that. We spread twenty-three documents over the four picnic table tops. He began walking around each concrete picnic table carefully examining each signature. Taking his time, he looked at each document carefully. He didn't make two full circles around the tables before he reached over and picked up one of the documents with a signature on it then looked at me as he flung it to the ground and said, "This is a forgery, and it's damn poor forgery at that!"

The document he had determined was a forgery was the document with Judge Burns's signature on it that denied our motion to reconsider our motion for a new trial. It was the one dated February 4, 2000, but not filed in the clerk's office until February 14, 2000 (two days after Judge Burns had passed away). For me, that was very convincing evidence. I considered that old man a true expert witness. He didn't even know why we were examining the signatures and had no dog in the fight. I didn't think it possible to find anyone more expert than him.

I didn't really believe Descusio, the AUSA, had done the dirty deed. He was too smart for that. I didn't really expect Agent March had done the deed either for the same reason, although I did consider him to be corrupt, dirty, and sleazy. But who did? I just couldn't figure out why it was so important to them that Kara and I remain in prison, especially if we were really innocent. Why would they go to all this trouble?

Paul and Phillip seemed to be just as impressed and convinced by the inmate's evaluation of our documents. Together we made a decision to contact a handwriting expert to check on examining the document to make a professional, legal conclusion about it. Paul and Phillip took a couple of the blown-up documents along with the document in question and visited a handwriting expert. The expert took out an eyepiece and looked carefully at the signatures blown up on the 8 1/2 by 14 inch paper. He said it appeared suspicious to him just on first glance.

He agreed to examine the signatures more carefully and even testify to what he might find. He wanted four thousand dollars for the work. He was commonly called by the government to testify on their behalf in cases. His credentials were impeccable. The agreement was made that we would hire him (I still don't know where the money was going to come from). There was only one provision. He had to examine the *original* document in order to testify truthfully. Phillip assured him that would be no problem. The federal system allowed such examinations by experts in criminal cases. The document should be available in the clerk's office, and the examination would have to occur in the federal building in an area provided by the clerk of court.

It was encouraging. A forged document would just further add to all the misconduct, fraud, perjury, and other crazy things connected to our case. Phillip and Paul left his office downtown and went straight to the clerk's office. They showed the clerk the faxed copy of the decision that Phillip had and told her they wanted to look at the original document from the folder holding the information about my case. She went to the file room to retrieve the document while they waited. She came back in later with two pages, one from my file folder and one from Kara's file folder. When she laid them down, it was obvious to Phillip and Paul that both documents were just copies and not original.

Phillip told her, "No, I need the original document. We plan on bringing in an expert tomorrow to examine the document. He needs to see the original for the examination to be legal and binding. He can't testify about his findings unless his examination is of the original document."

She said, "I understand that, but, Mr. Watson, that's all there is. There is no other copy in either Phillips's folder."

Phillip said, "Well, there has to be an original document. Let me ask you another question. Who filed this motion with your office?"

She answered, "I have no idea. I went to lunch and came back and it was in my box (she pointed to a small letter holder type tray on the counter). I guess the judge's secretary filed it."

Phillip just looked at her and Paul and then said, "I know the judge's secretary, Mrs. Roberts. I'll just go and ask her if she filed it."

With that, Phillip turned and went through a door and down a hallway. The door was standing propped open. Paul watched Phillip walk down the hallway, stop in front of a door, and knock. Inside the office reception area behind a desk sat Mrs. Roberts. They exchanged greetings, and the secretary asked Phillip, "What can I do for you today, Mr. Watson?"

Phillip said, "Mrs. Roberts, I'd like you to look at this document and see if you might have filed it for Judge Burns with the clerk's office, if you don't mind. It's signed by Judge Burns, and the clerk thought you might have filed it."

She was speaking before she had even glanced at the document. She said, "Mr. Watson, unless it is dated before October 1, 1999, I didn't file it. I haven't filed anything for Judge Burns since he took his leave of absence on October 1." She looked at the document and said, "No, I did not file this. I have never seen this." Phillip thanked her and returned to the clerk's office.

Phillip told the Clerk, "Mrs. Roberts said she's never seen this document and definitely didn't file it."

The clerk said, "Well, I certainly don' know who did. As I said before, it was in my box there when I returned from lunch."

Paul spoke up and said, "Couldn't anyone have just come in off the street and stuck that in your box?"

She just laughed and said, "Well, I guess they could have. I'm sorry, I can't help you with this."

All this controversy just ratcheted up our suspicions regarding this document. We couldn't use the handwriting expert if there was no original document to examine. His testimony wouldn't even be allowed according to Phillip. It seemed to me the fact that no original document seemed to exist should have disqualified that document. According to a Rule 33 procedure rule, the clerk is not allowed to accept a document unless she can verify the document is legitimate and the signature is true. If she didn't know who filed it and the judge was already dead, how could she possible verify the signature? It seemed at every turn in our case, justice had been perverted, twisted, or circumvented.

In looking at the document, I found several more problems than I had even considered before. I had been so focused on the legitimacy of the signature I had probably missed some things previously. There was a line and a half typed at the very bottom of all the court documents I had in my possession. It had a blank in the top line to handwrite in a date regarding the filing of the motion. Occasionally, the line is not quite parallel with the bottom of the page, but the difference is only centimeters. However, on this document, those lines run across the bottom half of the page at a forty-five-degree angle. A typewriter could not possibly type at that angle. It dawned on me what the problem was. As a schoolteacher, I had cut and pasted thousands of documents. If I were cutting and pasting and didn't get something taped or glued down, it would move when I turned it over to copy. It was clear to me this typed line had been added to the document. However, it was not taped or glued down and slipped to that angle as the paper was turned over on the copy machine to copy. Evidently, whoever rigged this copy was in an awful hurry and didn't take the time to fix the document. I am sure they thought this was only a minor, unnoticeable problem. Only someone familiar with copying thousands of documents or papers would probably notice it, and I did.

I wondered, "Was the judge's signature taped on this document as well? Is that why it sits a good quarter of an inch above the line?" The evidence seemed overwhelming. This was a completely bogus document. That was the only conclusion a reasonable person could draw.

The final concern that kept gnawing at me was the time on the fax showing it had been faxed from the federal building clerk's office at 11:59 p.m. on a Monday night. This document was not automatically faxed and was physically faxed by someone in that office at that fax machine. Who would be in the federal building that closed at 5:00 p.m. at 11:59 p.m. at night faxing a document.? I remember

Paul couldn't get in after 5:00 p.m. to post my bond. Maybe the time on the machine was just wrong. No, because it was on Phillip's fax machine when he had arrived at work at 8:00 a.m. in the morning. It had been faxed overnight. It had been faxed at 11:59 p.m. from the clerk's office in the federal building. The question was, "What can we do about all of these irregularities?"

Chapter 29

Moving

The weeks following the judge's death and the denial to our motion were hard weeks for us all. Our fragile hope seemed to have been crushed, however, February still had one more surprise for us.

The last week of February 2000, Mrs. Stewart, the food service secretary/tech called me into her office and told me she had heard through the grapevine that I was going to be transferred. The Bureau of Prisons had a security point system. Without going into great detail, it meant that your security classification was based on this point system. I was at a medium-high facility because my security points were high. Not particularly because of the crime I had committed, but more because of the length of my sentence. The security point table had changed after I had gotten there and apparently had changed again. She said it was rumored I was now qualified to be at a low facility because of a drop in my security points and level.

Mrs. Stewart wanted to know if I was pleased or if I would be disappointed to leave. I told her I didn't want to leave. I was only about ten minutes from my brother. From my cell, I could see TV and tower lights next door to the house I had lived in. I was in Memphis, near home. She said since I would prefer to stay at FCI Memphis, she would ask the food service administrator to put a management variable on me. She said he could request one and claim there was an institutional need for me because of the significance of my work as the clerk in food service. She said my work was invaluable to the institution and the request would not be unreasonable or out of line.

A few days later my name came out on a callout for a team meeting. I showed up on time and was ushered into the inner hallway and then into a conference room where team meetings were held. Each inmate was to meet with his unit team every six months to update and review his progress in the system and to talk about any problems he may be having or any problems the institution may be having with him. I had not been to a team meeting since January of 1999. Somehow I had missed my first six-month team meeting. The unit team consisted of my counselor, a case manager, and the unit manager.

When I entered the room, the only face I recognized was Mr. Wren, my counselor. The unit manager and case manager were not the same ones I had seen thirteen months before. The new case manager, a man, and unit manager, a woman, introduced themselves to me.

The unit manager began by asking me if I was Jack Phillips. I said I was, and he asked me what I had done since my last team meeting. I told him I had gone through A and O, been assigned to Beale-8 Unit, been assigned to work in food service as a cook but had moved up to the clerk's job, and taught GED classes as well for the education department. He looked at me and said, "No, I mean what have you accomplished since your last team meeting six months ago?"

I told him I hadn't had a team meeting since the very first one in January 1999. He scolded me by saying, "That's not right!" He looked at Ms. Hart, the case manager, and said, "Look up and see when his last team meeting was."

She began thumbing through my file as he looked back and forth from me to her. I said to Mr. Russell, the unit manager, "Can I ask you something?"

He said, "Sure."

I said, "Who are you people? You weren't here the last time I was here."

He said he and Ms. Hart had been there nine months. I told him I had never seen either of them in my life. I told him the only one in the room I knew was Mr. Wren.

Ms. Hart looked up about that time and said, "He's right. He hasn't been in a team meeting since January 25, 1999."

The case manager looked surprised. He didn't have much to say to me after that. He told me the main purpose of the team meeting that day was for him to tell me I was going to be transferred to a low-custody facility. I told him I really didn't want to leave Memphis because all my family was in the Memphis area.

He said, "I' m sorry, Mr. Phillips. Your security points are simply too low for you to stay here. They are going to ship you out, and your transfer papers have already gone to region."

As soon as the meeting ended, I headed over to Mrs. Stewart's office. I told her, "They're going to ship me out if you can't stop it with a management variable."

She assured me she would get with the food service administrator and try to do just that. She told me not to worry because management variables were routinely given. A few hours later she announced over the intercom for me to report to her office in food service. I went in and she said, "Sorry, Jack. We tried, but we were too late. Region has already approved your transfer, and we can't stop it."

I thanked Mrs. Stewart and headed back to the unit. That old feeling of uncertainty and dread returned in full force. I told Keith. He was just as upset as I was. He didn't want to see me leave him behind again. While I was telling Keith and griping about it, Morgan Green came by the door and stepped into our cell. He said, "What's wrong?" I told him. He scowled at me and said, "Boy, quit bitching. When they send you to lower-classified joint, you should be glad. For one, it will be a better place than this higher-classification place, and two, it means you are just closer to the door. You go on to the low. The next stop will be the camp, then the halfway house, and then home. So quit complaining. None of us want to see you leave, but we'd rather see you go to a low than stay at a medium high. Do you understand?"

I said, "Yes, sir. But I am sure going to miss you guys."

I could see tears form in the eyes of this crusty old inmate. I knew it would be hard on Keith and Morgan too. I told Keith, "Now when I leave, keep your mouth shut and stay out of trouble. I wasn't gone from Mason two days before you were in the hole. Don't do that again, okay?"

Keith said, "I'll behave. I won't do anything stupid to get in trouble."

I told Morgan, "Keep an eye on him, will you? Just keep him out of trouble."

He said, "Don't worry, I'll watch out for his sorry ass."

About two days later, Morgan showed up at my door with tears streaming down his face. I jumped up and said, "What's wrong, Mr. Green?"

He told me, "Hell, you won't believe it, Jack. You were worried about leaving. They just called me in and said I'm going to the medical facility in Lexington, Kentucky, myself. I'm leaving tomorrow. Hell, I'm leaving before you do!"

I was greatly affected because I owed that man so much. He had taken me under his wing and taught me how to "do time." He did my laundry, watched my room, went to visits with me, and counseled me on every prison problem that came up. Now he was leaving.

He said, "I'll come over tonight so we can talk."

I responded, "You do that, Mr. Green. I'll be looking forward to it." He left, and shortly after Keith came back to the room. I told Keith about Mr. Green leaving. Keith's face even looked sadder. The two men he spent most of the time with were now both leaving him. There is a soul-wrenching sadness that hit's a person when an inmate friend leaves. Whether he's going home, going to a halfway house, or being transferred to another facility, it always leaves a lonely spot in a prisoner's life. That's a reality of prison that only inmates experience. The loneliness is bottomless.

That night Mr. Green came by the room. Keith was in the day-room watching TV, and I was glad. It gave Mr. Green and me time to talk. I told him, "Look, Mr. Green, I want to talk to you about something really serious."

He said, "Okay."

I told him, "I don't want tomorrow to be the last time I see you. I've come to love and respect you, as has my family. I know there's a great chance we won't meet again. However, my Christian faith has given me a real belief in eternal life. I know I am personally a sinner and as a result deserve death, but God sent his Son, Jesus Christ, who lived a perfect life and died on the cross taking my sin and your sin and the sin of the world with him. He took our punishment. He paid for all our sins and justified us before God. I know I have eternal life because I have accepted his sacrifice for me and accepted him as Lord and Savior. Mr. Green, all you have to do is believe in your heart that he died for your sin too. All you have to do is accept that you're a sinner and couldn't pay the debt yourself. You have to repent your sins and ask him to save you and come into your life. You must believe that God resurrected him and that he lives today. You have to confess him before men, and he will confess you to the Father. Mr. Green, your salvation is just a matter of faith. If you will believe, you will have eternal life too, and we can see each other again and spend all eternity together in his presence."

I had never been so bold at expressing my faith. I believe if Mr. Green had heard that from anyone else, he would have probably given them a cussing and walked out. But I knew something. I knew Mr. Green loved me as much as I loved him.

A tear leaked out of his right eye and ran down his face. He just looked at me and nodded. I said, "Will you at least think about it, Mr. Green?"

He said, "I will, Jack. I'll sure think about it."

The next morning at 6:05 a.m., Mr. Green knocked at my cell door. He had his duffel bag strap thrown over his shoulder with his meager possessions. I told him to come in. Mr. Green looked at me and smiled the biggest smile I had ever seen on his face. It was a really genuine smile. He came in and stuck out his hand, and as we shook hands and hugged each other, he said, "Jack, you know what we talked about last night? We'll, I've taken care of that. I accepted Jesus."

I had pure joy rush through my soul. It was a rush of pure happiness. Tears streamed down my face. He cried too. We hugged and hugged. We told each other goodbye, but we also said we would see each other again. It might not be in this life, but we would see one another again and for all eternity.

I was transferred on March 21, 2000. Keith and I had to say goodbye again.

Chapter 30

March 21, 2000

I was called to report with my property to R and D (Receiving and Departure) at 8:00 a.m. on March 21, 2000. I had already mailed three large boxes with my legal work, my personal papers, and books to my brother because I could only take a minimal amount of items.

At eight forty-five, I was shackled and put in the back of a van with three other inmates. Once again, our destination was the auxiliary airstrip at Memphis Airport. Buses and other vans arrived. A few were empty, but most carried prisoners. I knew the routine. There was a large US Marshal presence too. Just like before they wore all black and flak jackets. They carried automatic rifles and shotguns. Most had sidearms in holsters on their belts. They established a large perimeter around the area.

Everyone was in waiting mode. We were all waiting for the airplane the inmates had labeled Con Air. Last time when I had been brought here from Mason, I was loaded on a van and went to FCI Memphis. I did not board the plane then, but I felt certain this time I would board the plane For Oklahoma City and the transit center there (the same one Kara had been to). I had heard the horror stories about the place, but Kara didn't describe it as being that bad.

Eventually the plane did arrive. For a moment it looked like mass confusion. Men and women prisoners disembarked buses and vans and stood in line on the tarmac near their respective vehicles while stairs were placed up against the plane to an obscure door. Inmates begun coming off the plane and forming their own line on the tarmac.

Near each line of men was an officer with a clipboard. The only thing more plentiful than clipboards were guns. Somehow the officers seemed to make sense of it all.

Finally, my name was called. I was prepared to head to the airplane like the other men on my van had done. However, I was pulled out of line and placed on a large bus marked Forrest City. That bus was almost full; in fact, there was only one sent for me. My shackles had been exchanged with officers from Forrest City, and I took my seat next to a four-hundred-pound man. I was smashed between him and the side of the bus.

I knew Forrest City Arkansas was only fifty-three miles from the Memphis bridge, but when we crossed the Mississippi River, it seemed five hundred miles away. They passed out our sack lunches. Each bag contained a sandwich, an apple, and a plastic bag of liquid Kool-Aid. When I am shackled, I almost have to be a contortionist to reach my mouth. I tried to eat. Some men gave up and just dropped theirs to the bus.

When we reached the prison, I was shocked at the enormity of it. The Memphis compound was small compared to this place. There were only about 900 inmates at FCI Memphis when I was there. Here, the housing units were really large 2-story brick buildings. There were three of these large buildings. Each contained four housing units. There were Marianna A and B (both downstairs) and Marianna C and D (both upstairs). There were also a Helena Unit and A Wynne Unit all with A, B, C, and D units like Marianna. A total of twelve units. I figured there must be 1,500 men there. It was also spread out over a lot more space. Of course, we were in the country here, with farmland all around the institution at Forrest City.

We were unloaded, almost forty of us, and taken to R and D and crammed into three small holding cells. Before they closed the doors, they called out about a dozen men and told them they would be moving down the road about a half a mile to the prison camp. That must have been good because they were all smiling. They said the rest of us would be processed into FCI Forrest City Low even though this facility was still behind a double chain-link fence with the rolled barbed wire on top.

It took the rest of the day to process us into the facility. We had interviews with medical and psychiatric staffs. Some of the men were called out and taken away to their assigned units. Evidently they had already been here and were taken away and now returning. By 4:00 p.m. there were only eight of us left. We were locked in the holding cells and counted. After count, they unlocked the door and told us to follow them. I was ready to get to my unit. I was still upset that I had to leave Memphis, and the day was wearing on me. The facility was a dull gray and extremely depressing and foreboding. My journey was getting darker.

Chapter 31

In the Hole

When we were shackled and escorted out of R and D onto the compound the three menacing-looking units were about one hundred yards north straight ahead across the compound. I was wondering which unit I would be going to. They bad signs on them with their names (from left to right, Wynne, Marianna, and Helena). Wynne was closest to the rec yard. Helena was closest to the cafeteria. Marianna was an equal distance from both. From where we stood, we could see sidewalks snaking across the compound, with at least one sidewalk going up to each unit from the center of the compound.

To my surprise, we didn't head across the compound. We went west along the sidewalk by the building and not north toward the units. We approached a metal door at a two-story building, which wasn't nearly as large as the housing units. The sign on the door told us all we needed to know. It read Segregated Housing Unit. Why were we going to the hole?

None of the inmates with me said anything. We all just stood there. I didn't know if they realized what was happening. I did. I said, "Officer, why are we going to the hole?"

He turned and looked at me and said, "Because there is no room in the housing units for you men. It's full. You'll be housed here until we find room for you in the units."

I know my face must have lit up red! Here I was in a place I didn't want to be after leaving a place I wanted to stay, and the new place didn't really even have room for me! This was crazy! I hadn't broken a rule or committed any kind of infraction to be going to the hole. Here I was after this horrible day being put in the hole not for something I did or didn't do but because the institution had more inmates than they had rooms.

They put is into small holding cells again. We were told to strip down naked. There we were, eight grown, naked men crammed together in a small holding cell. They passed out prison jumpsuits, underwear, T-shirts, socks, and flat tennis shoes to us through a hole in the bars of the holding cells. We were given a towel, washcloth, small toiletry bag, a sheet, a thin bedspread, and a thin pillow. All the toiletry items said Bob Barker on them. I guess *The Price Is Right* was not his only source of income.

When we were dressed, our names were called and our cell numbers assigned. We were handcuffed again and escorted to our cells. I was taken to a downstairs cell and placed in one by myself. With the upstairs cells, I guess the hole could handle about 160 men. I don't know how many were occupied, but I assumed most were.

At about 5:45 p.m., the guards opened my door and placed another man in the cell with me. His name was Cliff Toombs. Cliff said he had just self-surrendered. He was a forty-year old white man who was a farmer from Arkansas. I thought I could smell the farm on him, but soon learned what I was sensing from Cliff was fear. I had already spent about twenty months incarcerated. Also, I was coming down in security from a medium high to a low. This was his first prison experience. He was frightened beyond words. In fact, he was almost petrified.

At about 6:00 p.m., it got dark outside and dark in our cell too. When I tried to turn on the light, nothing. I stopped an officer passing by and told him our light wasn't working. He said he knew it, but it was broken, and there was nothing he could do. I asked him to move us to another cell, but he said all the cells were full. I didn't mind the darkness too much at first, for I knew I would probably sleep better in the total darkness. But Cliff was about to lose it. He told me he had eight years to do, but he said, "I can't do eight years in the total darkness. I just can't!" I tried to assure him he wouldn't have to do any of his time like this. He had a lot of questions for me that night.

By the fifth day of darkness, I had had about enough myself. I wanted out as much as Cliff. I was so angry, completely furious. In the hole, men kick the metal doors and rattle pipes and scream and holler all day and all night. They scream to their friends on the far ends of the hall. It never stopped. The officers paraded up and down the halls with their keys rattling, their radios blaring, and them talking and laughing at the top of their lungs. They yelled back and forth with and at the inmates. I was angry about leaving Memphis. I was angry about being in Forrest City. I was angry about being in the hole. I was angry about being in the dark. I was angry about not being able to call home or write or mail letters. I was angry because I had not been able to communicate with the family. I was angry because I had not received a piece of mail yet in Forrest City. I was angry!

The sixth day, early in the morning, an inmate trustee/electrician and his guard escort showed up at our cell door. The guard handcuffed Cliff and me and had us step out of the cell. The inmate worker was carrying a small ladder and wearing a tool belt. They told us they were there to "fix the light." Cliff and I watched as they simply replaced the light bulb! The light itself had never been broken. It just needed a new bulb. They had let us sit in the hole in the dark all that time when all they had to do was replace the light bulb. I just knew I was going to love this place!

On March 28 (my son's birthday), we were released from the hole and taken to laundry to receive our prison clothes and bedding so we could be processed into a unit. Cliff was assigned to Wynne D. I was assigned to Marianna D. It was an upstairs unit. The door to the unit faced east, toward Memphis. I would be there for the next eight years.

Chapter 32

FCI Forrest City
Getting Started

FCI Forrest City Low was significantly different from FCI Memphis Medium High. For one thing, we weren't housed in cells with strong metal doors. We were housed in what were called cubes. They had a short three-foot wall in front with an opening to walk through. The opening was about the width of a small door space. The three-foot wall rose up on each side to a height of about five feet then extended to the back wall. The ceiling in the building was about 30 feet up. It was an open cube. They ran the length of the building on both sides and had four more rows grouped together 2-by-2 in the middle. Each unit was designed to hold about 120 men. There were game rooms and small TV rooms located across from the counselor offices in each unit. However, these game rooms had been converted into living quarters. There were about ten bunks in each small room and about fifteen bunks in the larger rooms. The units now could easily accommodate 160–180 men. We also had a laundry room with washers and dryers. Only one small room remained that was used as a TV room. While I was there, these rooms would also be converted to living quarters. The number of inmates rose to over 2,000 at Forrest City Low. It was overcrowded as were all the BOP facilities. Memphis, which had 900 when I left, had triple bunked and now had over 1,300.

The first thing I did after my initial team meeting was submit a cop-out to work in education. I attended A and O and got that over with and was trying to land a job. Before I heard anything, I was assigned to food service. There were over three hundred workers in this food service. When I reported, the cook foreman had a clipboard and checked my name off as I went through the door. I wasn't told what my job was or where I was supposed to work in the food service department. I looked all over and came to the front dish room. It was large and located just inside and between the two front doors. Inmates just pushed their dirty trays through the windows after eating, and the dish room cleaned them and all the plastic utensils. I saw a man I had known at Mason sorting and handling the plastic utensils. He told me to just help him. I did. I worked each day and just left when my shift ended.

I worked there for about two weeks and was never told anything by any staff member in food service. The second week, I wrote another cop out and walked it over to education myself. I talked first to a male staff member (a teacher) and then an assistant supervisor of education (a female). They listened to my spiel, interviewed me, and hired me on the spot. They escorted me back to an office to meet my new boss. The office was in the back of a classroom. They introduced me to lady named Ms. Gill. She was a black lady and happened to be the wife of my counselor, Mr. Gill. She was in charge of the GED classes. Other staff members were in charge of the pre-GED classes and others in charge of the literacy GED classes. The literacy class was for those who tested in the range from can't read at all to third-grade level. The pre class was from fourth- to sixth-grade level. The GED classes were for those who tested from seventh grade up.

That day the students in her class were taking the practice GED test. It was an official practice test. If they passed it, they could take the real GED test. Ms. Gill told me before she could hire me I would have to take the practice test myself and show her what I knew. I didn't want to take the test. I told her I have a master's degree, but I haven't had a test in twenty-five years! I took the test. I finished all five parts in about an hour and a half. When I took the finished test to her, she said, "You need to finish it. All of it." I told her I was finished. She informed me that it was four-hour test and that I could not possibly have finished it in an hour and a half.

She began grading my answer sheet with a stencil. I saw over her shoulder that I had not missed a question on the first test (science) or the second test (social studies). I had gotten the first fifty questions all right. As she graded the reading test, she switched stencils. She turned around smiling and looked at me and said, "Look, you didn't do well on the reading or the science or the social studies tests." I smiled back at her and said, "I think if you use the right stencil, the one you were using first, you will find I got all the reading questions right, like I did the science and social studies tests." She just roared with laughter! I missed two questions in math and got all the language questions right as well. She said, "Mr. Phillips, you are hired. Welcome to the education department."

Chapter 33

Teaching GED Classes

The same day I was hired to work in education, I met Mr. John Lawton. Mr. Lawton was a retired superintendent from the local school district. In fact, he had been a teacher, a coach, a principal, and the superintendent. He now worked for the local vocational college, who volunteered him to the institution. He was a veteran, a former college football player, a former high school coach, and a great math teacher. He and I hit it off immediately. We had other tutors that worked in our classroom, but they were all gone by the end of 2000, and it was just Mr. Lawton and me. During that school year, we had 212 graduates and led the nation's Bureau of Prison programs in number of graduates that included over 100 institutions.

In addition, Ms. Gill, the lady that hired me and oversaw the GED program for the institution, left and went across the street to be education camp coordinator at the camp facility, much like a college campus. Our new supervising teacher was an attractive early thirties petite blond lady named Ms. Hill. Ms. Hill would be my boss for the next three years. We led the nation those next three years with 205, 198, and 195 graduates. We had a tremendous working relationship. I was so fortunate to be able to work with Ms. Gill, Ms. Hill, and Mr. Lawton. All three were professional and only interested in educating the men that passed through our classes. Overtime I earned their respect and was soon elevated to grade 1 pay. We had three classes a day back then, and they were all full, about thirty men per class. The assistant supervisor of education at the low, Ms. Yount, was exceptional too and pushed the testing. It was a successful formula.

In addition to the GED classes, we also had pre-OED classes and literacy classes. The literacy class had men that scored between 0 and third grade on the placement test. The pre-GED class had men that cored between fourth and sixth grade on the placement test. The GED classes were made up of men who scored seventh grade and above on the placement test. Congress had enacted education that required men with no high school diploma to be working on their GED or risk losing good time credit. Besides the nine to one hundred men in the GED classes, there were another nine to one hundred in the Pre-GED classes and fifty to sixty in the literacy classes. It was a real school with hundreds of students. The leisure library and the law library were also contained within the department. It was a very busy place. My hours were from 7:30 a.m. until 3:30 p.m. Monday–Friday. I felt extremely fortunate to be working in my professional area. I had more education and teaching experience than any of the Bureau of Prison staff. It wasn't long before I was administering tests, grading, recording, and keeping testing records for all students. I did everything but administer the official GED test. I also typed all the monthly rosters and typed the pay sheets for the more than seventy-five inmates that worked in the department. I settled into that routine, and time flew by.

Chapter 34

Legal Questions

Kara and I were both still reeling from the forged denial had received in regard to our evidentiary hearing. Paul and Phillip Watson were working furiously to prepare for our direct appeal to the United States Sixth Circuit Court of Appeals in Cincinnati, Ohio.

Paul had met a strange man at the bookstore where he worked part-time. The man indicated and gave every impression that he had worked in the CIA at some point. He too became a friend and wanted to help once he heard our story. Paul was soon hearing strange noises on his telephone. In fact, it was ringing at strange hours in the middle of the night, and no one would be on the other end of the line. He began to notice telephone-marked vans parked just down from his house on the street and often in the driveways of empty houses but never actually saw anyone get in or out of the vans. Eventually he told our mystery man about it and asked if he could find out if his phones were tapped. The man claimed he had a device and asked Paul to call a specific number. The mystery man called back immediately and said the phones were indeed tapped. Phillip Watson was skeptical about it.

However, it wasn't long before Phillip began to suspect that his telephones at his offices were tapped, as well as his home phones too. Phillip brought in a professional to sweep his office and check his phones. He found not only had his office and home phones been tapped, but he found a bug in his office and realized his office was tapped. He even found a tracking device under the bumper of his wife's car. Paul dropped by the office one day, and Phillip gave him the shush sign and motioned for Paul to follow him. They went outside and talked in the parking lot near a busy highway in hushed tones. Phillip told Paul about the tracking device and office bug he had discovered.

For about two months, Phillip Watson was not available. His partner said he was out of town, but he didn't know where and had no phone number to call him. In fact, he said the only one that knew where Phillip and his wife and children were with Phillip's father. As it turned out, Phillip had taken his family secretly to Europe. The tapping and tracking devices had put fear in Phillip's heart for family and himself.

A few months later, Phillip returned. He would not talk about where he had been or why he had left. He said to just "let it go." After showing up at the low for a lawyer's visit that spring, we began planning for our direct appeal to the Sixth Circuit Court of Appeals. We went through the motion and began arranging our exhibits for the accompanying appendix. At one of those visits, as we were finishing up the motion, Phillip asked me for a copy of the letters from the AUSA in Missouri to Nance and Tisdale's lawyer stating that Terry Descusio had promised their clients (Nance and Tisdale) a deal to testify against Jack Phillips. Phillip said he couldn't locate his letters, so I gave him my copies and told him those were my last two copies. He assured me he had copies at the office and would send me new ones. We labeled all the exhibits with the appropriate letters and numbers with a nonerasable black laundry pen. We were only raising a few key points in our appeal.

- We had challenged the drug amounts based on Mike Field's evidentiary hearing testimony that only six to eight ounces of meth was cooked at the cook on May of 1997 instead of the two pounds that Nance had claimed was cooked. If we could just win that point, it would knock five years off my sentence and three years off Kara's sentence because of the mandatory minimums that were based on drug amounts. It seemed clear we would win that argument. Fields even accounted for his three ounces.

- We were objecting that the witnesses had deals and that they and the prosecutor had lied about the deals at trial and at sentencing. We had produced the letters and the proffer agreements at the evidentiary hearing and they were now part of the record (as were the Rule 35s).
- We were arguing they had lied about their arrests and convictions.
- We were arguing a Brady violation regarding Mike Fields. (They had his statement, which was exculpatory evidence, and they were required by law to tum in over but still had not done so.)
- We argued a Jencks violation because they had not turned over Tisdale's statement to us prior to trial and denied it existed (it had turned up in our PSR prior to sentencing).

Our direct appeal was filed in early 2001, under the year deadline we had since the evidentiary hearing ruling. Phillip moved his law practice to the suburbs and shared an office complex with another attorney. He had parted ways with his original partner.

Both Paul and Phillip were reluctant to even mention our case on the phone or in Phillip's office. They met and talked the most about the case at church. They also met at bookstores and cafes. Phillip had not been the same since his return from Europe. He was fearful about any and everything.

The mystery man got weirder and weirder. At one point, he wanted Paul to fly to Washington, DC, on a private plane to met with some people. Keith Hawkins, my old cellmate, convinced Paul not to get on a private plane like that. He advised Paul to tell the mystery man he would go to DC to meet the people, but he would only fly on a commercial airliner. The mystery man had now been around for over a year. After Paul refused the private plane, Paul never saw him again. He heard from him once after he had been arrested for shoplifting. He had called Paul to see if Phillip would represent him. Phillip was so suspicious about him and everything else he said he would think about it. A few days later, the feds arrested the mystery man. He told Phillip that Descusio was behind it. He was extradited to Texas for something there. The only thing we ever heard from him was that it was just part of his cover. We never learned his real identity (assuming the name, George Jones, he gave us was fake), nor did we ever learn whom he really worked for.

Chapter 35

Chaplain Services

One of the most important things I did upon my arrival at FCI Low Forrest City was get involved in the chaplain department. I got involved in the services and became close friends with one of the chaplains.

The supervising chaplain was a stoic, late-middle-aged black female named Ms. Rambo. I call her stoic because she never changed her expression or raised or lowered her monotone voice. She seemed introverted. Chaplain Rambo knew the Bible, and I felt she was doctrinally sound. Although I didn't interact with her much, I enjoyed her sermons.

There were two other chaplains. One of the two, Chaplain Crosby, had arrived about the same time as I did. New to the facility and to prison ministry, it was his first job as a prison chaplain. He was younger than I but had gone to seminary and started his public ministry later than most pastors. Previously he had been the pastor of a large Baptist church. Much to his surprise, a group of members and some of his supposed friendly deacons had met secretly and eventually ran him off. He was wounded deeply by the betrayal and scarred by the whole affair.

Chaplain Crosby had a wife and three young sons. Having grown up in rural Mississippi, he was the product of a broken home and raised partially by his grandparents. He had been a good high school football player and loved the game. Of course, that was a common bond we had right off the bat.

Chaplain Crosby and I spent hours in his office talking about everything. Some days he would come through an adjoining door to the education department and tell Ms. Hill he needed to see me. She would excuse me from work and allow me to go with him to his office. He was a graduate of Dallas Seminary, and we felt the same about religious issues. He was really bitter about the treatment he had received at his first/last pastor experience. He would bring it up in almost all his sermons.

There was a more remarkable aspect to his being there. It had almost cost him his marriage. At one point, his wife was ready to leave him if he took the prison chaplaincy job. His preacher friends all ridiculed him for even considering becoming a prison chaplain. They pointed out churches that needed pastors, and he needed a big church. He applied for some of the openings but never got a good reception from any of them.

In his heart, Chaplain Crosby knew the Lord had called him into the prison ministry. He related that to his wife and to all those who opposed his taking the chaplain job. They just could not accept that the Lord would call him or anyone to such a ministry.

When Chaplain Crosby arrived at the institution, we averaged about ninety to one hundred at the services. Diverse volunteers came in about every night of the week from every denomination in the area.

As Chaplain Crosby overcame his bitterness and let the past go, he became more and more effective. The chapel seated about three hundred, but there was a sliding curtain in the back that could open up another entire area expanding the seating capacity to about six hundred. By the end of Chaplain Crosby's first year, when he preached on Sunday, the curtain was pulled back, and still there was standing-room only. The average congregation contained more than six hundred men. We had monthly communion, and many men were saved and baptized in a portable baptismal. Hundreds and hundreds of men made professions of faith. Men's lives were forever changed under Chaplain Crosby's ministry there. By every standard, his ministry there was a huge success.

Chaplain Crosby also officially sanctioned the Bible study classes I was holding in the unit. Without such authorization, my Bible-study group could have been shut down. He was a great source of information and encouragement to me personally. He brought clarity to my understanding of scriptural knowledge and helped me grow spiritually and accept my circumstances. I was so fortunate to meet a chaplain like him and have him become a close personal friend (just when I needed one the most).

In late 2001, it was announced that Chaplain Rambo would be leaving. We all assumed Chaplain Crosby would be the new supervising chaplain. After Chaplain Rambo left, Chaplain Crosby ran the department and functioned as the supervising chaplain. The chaplain department was understaffed before. The other chaplain was a forty-something fiery black preacher. He was a wonderful man too. They hired a third chaplain, a younger black man, but he left after only a few months.

They eventually hired a new supervising chaplain, a female named Chaplain Richardson. They passed over Chaplain Crosby. The new chaplain was a nice lady but could just never connect with the male inmates there. She had seniority on Chaplain Crosby and Chaplain Foster. The chaplain department employed about thirty inmates as clerks, orderlies, and church librarians. Inmates on the compound soon discovered that most of the inmates that worked in the chapel were either gay or child molesters. It was a dumping ground for inmates with that kind of character. It did great harm to the witness of the Christian community there. The attitude by the staff was, "Well, they have to work somewhere."

Chapter 36

Softball

I immediately got involved in the softball program. I was asked to teach a class for umpires because we had over thirty men who umpired in the program. Attendance at the umpire classes were mandatory if an inmate wanted to umpire in the official games. Officially, I was titled the stat man. That meant I also trained all the scorekeepers. I assigned them to work the various games. The umpires made a dollar a game, and the scorekeepers made fifty cents a game. I made twenty-five dollars a month for being the stat man.

The softball season lasted from March until October. I started my classes in February. There were actually two leagues: the A League and the B League. There were twelve teams in each league or twenty-four teams total. Games were played on two fields on Thursday nights, Friday nights, Saturday afternoons and Saturday nights, and Sunday afternoons and Sunday nights. We played twenty-four games each weekend. I had to assign scorekeepers for all the games. I also worked with the (inmate) commissioner and ended up scheduling all the games and assigning umpires as well. I usually played two games in the league and umpired as many as ten other games each weekend. With the twenty-five dollars for being the stat man and the money I made umpiring and scorekeeping, I easily made sixty to sixty-five dollars a month from the recreation department. It was profitable, enjoyable, and time-consuming.

As a player, the first summer I was there our unit team went 3–29! We had two inmate coaches in our unit that were lousy coaches and worse players. Two of the three games we won were actually forfeits, so I couldn't wait for the season to end and the draft league to begin. After I was drafted, I played on a team that won the draft league championship. I had always been good at placing the ball, and soon I had mastered hitting the big slow softball. With a .787 average, I led the league in hitting.

It wasn't uncommon to have five hundred to six hundred men at our weekend games. You've never seen a more brutal crowd than prison inmates. They showed no mercy to any player. The taunting and jeering from the crowd made grown men blush. They hooted and hollered on every error, every strikeout, and every bad play. Because of the instigation of the crowd, the games were very competitive and intense. Games and plays were talked about all over the compound for weeks after they had been played. You could quickly become a legend if you were a good player.

Beginning in 2001, I was asked to play on the White Boy Team. I had no idea what that meant. I learned it was a select team made up of only white players. There was also a Black Team, a Mexican Team, and a Caribbean Team. All these teams were good. Only the best players in the A League played on these teams. These teams played two games on Tuesdays. The losers played the first game on Wednesday, and the winners played the second game on Wednesday. Over the course of the summer, I would play in sixty or so league games and at least forty White Boy games. I was playing in over one hundred games each summer. I was right at fifty years old and would play softball into my near sixties.

Only the best players played in these select Tuesday and Wednesday games. There were former major league players and minor league players, former college basketball players, and even some former pro football players. There were some truly great softball players that loved to play the game. In these games, there were always great defensive plays, great throws, great base running, great hitting, and real drama. There was also much betting on these games.

The first game I played on the White Boy Team was against the Black Team. I pitched. Both teams were outstanding. Before the game as the teams warmed up, I began listening to all the conversations around me about bets and wagers on the game. I actually saw two Hispanic men shake hands and make a seven-thousand-dollar bet. There were many one-hudred-dollar bets. I estimated the betting at least thirty thousand dollars for that one game! There must have been a thousand inmates at these Tuesday and Wednesday games. Fans rooted for teams they bet on and along racial lines.

What pressure in a game! If you made a crucial error or failed to get a hit at a critical time, the thought was that he must have been paid off. Treachery was a way of life in prison. It wasn't out of the realm of possibility in a big-money softball game. We won the game that day, and I played my best softball in those big games. It was rare I would ever walk a batter, and I hit over .800 in those games. Our winning percentage was well over 90 percent. We almost always played the second game on Wednesdays (the game reserved for Tuesday's winners).

During the softball seasons, I suffered broken fingers on my right hand after being hit by batted balls but never went to medical. I knew my fingers were broken each time. I actually broke my little finger after being hit by a balls in one of the Tuesday/Wednesday games and saw the bone sticking out of my skin. I popped it back in place. Thank God I never broke an arm or leg. There were plenty of those playing prison softball.

Chapter 37

Kara

Kara was at FCI Carswell in Fort Worth, Texas. She started her time there in the low facility. That meant it had the double concertina wire on top of the double chain-link fences and even in between the fences. One of the first things Kara noticed was all the pigeons on the compound with no toes. They cut their toes off on the razor wire on and between the fences. Eventually, Kara was moved to the camp at Carswell (which was also a military base with a hospital).

At the camp, Kara found herself living in what had been married couples housing on the base. She lived in the duplex with four other women. They had a kitchen with real utensils and a microwave and a living room with their own remote-controlled TV. Eventually, Kara was on a specially chosen work detail with a handful of other female inmates that were bussed across the air force base to clean up in one of the base office buildings.

As a result, they did have contact with male military personnel that worked in the buildings. At least one of the inmates turned up pregnant. Some of the female inmates hustled the men for cigarettes or other contraband. All in all, they were well treated.

Kara liked the facility. From where she lived, she could not even see a fence. There was a lake on the property and a movie theater the inmates were allowed to use on certain nights.

One privilege they had was they could use their ID cards in vending machines strategically placed around the compound at both the low and the camp. It was unnecessary for her to purchase sodas and snacks at the commissary. Men never had that privilege at any of their facilities.

Once a year, in the summer, was family day. An inmate's family could visit, eat in a picnic setting with their family members, and move around the compound together. This was only at the camp, of course. It was almost like a summer block party held in many neighborhoods in America. They cooked out hamburgers and hot dogs and made a real enjoyable day of it.

Kara was involved in crocheting and other classes in the recreation department. She stayed busy and was relatively happy there. Her only real problem was her distance from Memphis and our family. It was rare that our family members could find the time or money to visit very frequently. If she got two visits a year, she was lucky. I know how it was tragic and unfair. She needed to see everyone and have hugs and kisses with those she loved—her brothers and sister, her mother, our children, and our grandchildren.

During her time there, her older brother had a severe stroke and was bedridden at her mother's house. Her younger brother had a bad case of muscular dystrophy, and he too was bedridden at her mother's house. Her mother was showing her age and having medical problems of her own. Her only surviving sister was diagnosed with muscular dystrophy, as was her sister's son. They also lived in Rector.

Because of all the illnesses and the distance from home, Kara decided she wanted to transfer closer to home. She hoped to see her family and our family more often. Also, the prison she chose had a dog training program. Kara loved dogs and wanted to get into that program. She would put in for that transfer as soon as she was eligible.

Chapter 38

Dad

I thought I was adjusting pretty well to prison life and to our circumstances; however, life is not static, and mine was soon to change.

Thomas Lloyd Phillips was the finest man I ever knew. Born in 1925, he was certainly my hero. He also happened to be my father. At eighteen, he was drafted, and at nineteen, he was fighting the Germans in World War II.

Wounded in the Battle of the Bulge, he was awarded three bronze stars, one with three clusters. His service was a defining moment in his life. Upon his release from the service, he took a job with the Arkansas-Missouri Power Company as a serviceman until he could find something better. He held that job for thirty-nine years before retiring.

By the time trouble came to our door, he was in his seventies, and his health was failing. He had visited me a few times in Memphis and even a few times in Forrest City at the low facility. He had been confined to a wheelchair and was only a shell of the man he had been physically.

On November 22, 2000, just three days before his seventy-fifth birthday, he passed away at 3:30 p.m. in the hospital. At about three o'clock that day, Paul had asked him, "Dad, are you hurting anywhere? Are you all right?"

Dad had answered, "No, I am not hurting, and I am fine."

Paul sat down in the chair in the hospital room and dozed off as dad dozed off in the bed. When Paul awoke, our dad had passed away. Apparently, he didn't suffer at all.

I had known dad was in the hospital again and that his health was not good. When I called home about five thirty, Paul gave me the news that our beautiful, lovely dad had passed away. I couldn't talk much. Paul explained to me that dad had not suffered.

About all I could think to say was to apologize to Paul for not being there. The shame that overcame me weakened my knees and brought tears to my eyes. I felt like I had let the man I loved the most down by not being there when he died. In my mind, I had let Mom down and, most of all, Paul. He was having to carry the burden on his own. I talked to Mom, and she was upset, but she was handling it just like I knew she would.

My entire family was Christian, and we believed in the resurrection of Jesus Christ and, subsequently, our own resurrection. My dad was a godly man bound for heaven. We knew without a doubt he was in the presence of the Lord and he would never suffer again. His mom and dad had both passed away, so he had real family on the other side.

As for me, I found it extremely hard to grieve. There was virtually no one to talk to except Chaplain Crosby. I went to his office as soon as I could. He just mainly let me talk about my dad. I cried some, and so did he. I was thankful to have a kind and caring friend.

I knew I would not be allowed to go to the funeral. I had seen other men try to attend family funerals, and it just did not happen at FCI Forrest City Low. I was hurting because I wouldn't be there for Mom, for Paul, for my dad's sister and her kids, and for my own children and grandchildren. How cruel it is not to be allowed to go to your father's funeral. I was miserable. The day of the funeral, I just went out and walked around the almost two-mile-long din track that circled the rec yard grieving for my dad. He had always been there for me, always. I hoped he had not died feeling ashamed of me.

I was allowed a call to Kara. It was the first in a couple of years. I wanted to tell her about Dad. She and I had dated since she was fourteen and married young. My dad had replaced her dad, who had passed away in 1981. She cried and was just as heartbroken as I and just as disappointed that she wouldn't be at the funeral either.

I was quickly coming to realize that things can and will often go from bad to worse. This dark cloud hung over me for months. I awoke many times in the middle of the night and ached and missed my dad. I knew I would never see him again in this world.

Chapter 39

Mom

A little less than two years later, on November 4, 2002, my mom, Mary Katherine Phillips, also passed away. Mom had been sick too. She seemed to really go downhill after dad passed away. However, I could just never envision her passing away.

Mom had come to visit me a few times since dad had passed away. I sensed a sadness about her and knew how much she must have missed him. I also saw she was suffering physically. Osteoporosis was taking its toll. We figured it had caused her some eighty broken bones over the past few years. Pain was her constant companion. She was also having breathing problems. The medical people explained to Paul that they could never give her CPR for fear of breaking all her ribs and sternum. She was really in constant pain.

Dad's death had been somewhat expected. Mom's death was not expected. I was asleep on my cot in cube 101, Marianna Delta, when a female lieutenant entered my cube and shook my bed and woke me up at about 2:30 a.m.

The officer said, "Wake up, Phillips."

I raised up and said, "Okay, what is it?"

She said, "You need to get dressed and come with me over to the lieutenant's office."

I said, "What for?"

She replied, "Just get dressed and come on."

They would often wake us up in the middle of the night and take us to the lieutenant's office for a UA (urine analysis) to test and see if we had been using drugs. It was not extraordinary that I was being awakened and told to go to the lieutenant's office.

I slipped on my sweatpants, tennis shoes, and coat. I was escorted to the lieutenant's office and told to sit down in a chair. About five minutes later, I was told to go down a hallway to the lieutenant's inner office. I knew then it wasn't a UA.

She looked at me and said, "Phillips, I am sorry, but I have some bad news."

I said. "Okay, what is it?"

She told me, "Your mom has passed away."

Once again I felt the numbing grief wash over me like a tidal wave. Once again, I felt ashamed. It was the shame I felt that hurt me so badly. I kept feeling like I had disappointed my mom. There is no one to share that feeling with; it is just too personal. First my dad, and now my mom. How much more could I take? I felt a real sense of abandonment and then was ashamed for thinking about myself. I shut that thought out of my mind. This wasn't about me. It was about my mom and my family.

The lieutenant asked me if there was anything she could do. I told her I would like to call my brother. She asked for the number and dialed it from the phone on her desk and then handed the receiver to me. Once again my brother's voice brought on that sense of shame. Again, Paul would have to handle this tragedy without me. He and Mom were closer than any son-mother I knew, and how badly he must be hurting and how alone he was feeling. Me gone, and Mom and Dad dead. My grief would also be greater because of my daughter, Mary Lynn, who loved Mother more than anyone on earth. I knew no one would miss Mary Katherine Phillips more than she. My son, Carey, and nephew, Abel, would be impacted by her death too. She had that kind of effect on everyone close to her. I wouldn't be there to comfort any of them, and they wouldn't be here to comfort me either. Again, I knew I wouldn't be allowed to go to the funeral. That hurt too.

I had never gone a week without speaking with my mom. All along in serving my sentence. I had called her once or twice a week. She had been such an encouragement. She had loved me unconditionally. Now I would never speak to Mom or Dad again, at least not in this world. I thought of recorded messages I had on my phone at home. I knew Ricky Short had taken my phone, and I was sure the messages had been erased. Just to hear her voice, even a recording, would have given me some comfort.

I grieved again for my father as a result. Grief for both of them overwhelmed me, and I was depressed for weeks but tried to function as if nothing had happened. I kept feeling like I had let everyone down. Had I been free, I would have been the one making all the funeral arrangements. That was just the way things fell on our family. Now, all that would fall to Mary Lynn and Paul and Jen.

There was another consideration. How would my family even pay for the funeral? Dad was a veteran, and his funeral was basically taken care of. Paul would be bearing the expense of Mom's funeral, and I knew he didn't have the money. Abel was in college, and Paul was stretched as thin as could be with that and with trying to support both Kara and me and even help our kids with their finances. Mom and Dad's home had been sold to pay off the debt for my lawyer and to help with their medical expenses. Although the funeral was only several thousand dollars, it was thousands Paul did not have. It would take him several years to pay off the debt. He could not even afford a tombstone. They would have a simple plaque in the ground with their name on it.

Now, of my original family, only Paul and I remained. I don't know how Paul handled all of it. The pressure of it all as well as the expense and the grief he felt was a great burden to carry alone. Of course, he had Jen, and she was a great support and comfort to him.

Paul continued to be faithful about visiting me every Saturday morning. It was sixty-plus miles each way, but he continued to make the drive. He even made trips to Fort Worth alone as well as with Mary Lynn and Carey to visit Kara.

Our family had been devastated by the loses of the patriarchs of our family. I believe I felt lonelier than I had ever felt before. I was finding it more and more difficult to keep from sliding over the abyss into a deep depression that may not have a way back. Furthermore, I found myself waking up frequently after dreaming about Mom and

Dad. I was familiar with the local cemetery in Rector, but I didn't know where they were buried. I dreamed of looking all over the cemetery for their plaques, but not being able to find them, I would end up running from grave site to grave site. I often woke up in a cold sweat wondering where they were buried. I asked for photos or a map, and everyone assured me they would send one, but no one ever got around to it, and the dreams (nightmares) continued for years.

Chapter 40

Loneliness

With Mom and Dad gone, loneliness consumed me. I guess it was closely related to depression. In fact, I couldn't and can't separate the two. I was more alone than ever. I could only really rely on Paul. My daughter had moved to Missouri. My son lived in Mississippi and worked at a large casino. Kara was still hundreds of miles away in Fort Worth, Texas. Mom and Dad were gone.

Paul and Jen both continued to come visit on Saturdays, and I had a cousin from Poplar Bluff, Missouri (my dad's niece), who also came once a month or so for a period of time. Other than that, no one came to visit. Later, my pastor, Brother John Henson, started visiting me once a month. Other than that, I saw no one. I bad been receiving six to eight letters a week the entire time I was incarcerated. Those letters stopped too. I guess the best example was Christmas. I would take out my address book, buy stamps and envelopes and cards, and mail out fifty or more Christmas cards. It was expensive. My return on the Christmas cards was not so good. The most I ever received was fourteen. It was pretty pathetic. Many inmates didn't receive any mail or Christmas cards at all, ever. After several years, there was a noticeable estrangement that had set in.

The nights in prison were the worst. They turned off the lights at about 10:00 p.m. I can't tell the number of nights I lay in that bed thinking about my past, the teaching and coaching and all the kids at school. My family. My wife. All the people that made my life rich. Where were my friends? God, how I missed them!

I ached and missed them then I would get mad at them for abandoning me. I stayed up all night writing them letters chastising them for abandoning me. Of course, I never mailed them. Each night was like the one before, lonely and long.

My phone calls became limited to one number, Paul's. My daughter was moving so often at the time I never had the right number. My son was too busy to talk, and no one else wanted to. I felt myself beginning to look inward. I was becoming more and more introverted, socially withdrawing. I had very little I wanted to say to anyone, and I didn't want to hear what anyone had to say much either. How could they know what I was going through? What was going on out there had very little to do with me.

I always had a *Commercial Appeal* newspaper subscription, thanks to Jen. I kept up with the events in Memphis, especially the sports, by reading the local paper. I was consuming paperbacks and novels and reading up to five books a week. I would rather read a book than talk. That just added fuel to my isolation and introversion. I was living with 1,800 men but was alone and lonely.

Chapter 41

2003–2004

I spent the winter of 2002 and 2003 grieving over the death of my mom and dad. So did Kara. My parents were like second parents to her. She had been with me since she was fourteen and had spent many, many days at our family home. I don't think a person ever gets over the death of a parent. However, one does learn you have to move on by getting up each day, bearing the grief and keeping alive.

I spent more time on my Bible studies. I was in the middle of writing seven thousand pages of handwritten notes on a Bible study for each book of the Bible. I had been consumed by it and was already teaching the first part as I finished up the remaining part. Studying, writing, and typing the Bible study was a three-year project of daily work. I was already teaching it in my unit when the chaplain asked me to teach it to the entire compound in a two-hour session on Saturday mornings in a room at the chapel. We averaged about sixty-five men each Saturday morning. It was a wonderful opportunity, and the entire process changed my life and my perspective. Eventually (because of 911), the chaplain department was ordered not to allow inmates to teach classes unless they could be in the room to monitor what taught. This was to prevent the Muslim community from radicalizing their members in their prison meetings, but it resulted in my chapel class being cancelled in the fallout. Years later they installed cameras in all the rooms so the chaplains could monitor the classes from television monitors in their offices. I continued the teaching the Bible study in my unit each night.

I also focused on the GED teaching. We continued graduating GED students at a record pace. However, changes were coming to the education department. Back in 2001, they had started building a medium-high facility to go along with the low and the camp. This would become a federal correctional compound with three facilities. It was finished and set to open in 2003. Ms. Hill, my boss and the architect of our success, decided to move to the education department at the new medium-high facility. She had gone through a divorce and then remarried. Her new husband worked in the facility department (plumbing) at the low. He was transferred to the medium high, so Ms. Hill decided to go there and work at the same facility as her husband. I understood, but I knew that the education department at the low would never be the same. Our number of graduates dropped the first year from one hundred ninety-five to one hundred twenty. For the first time in four years, we did not lead the nation in graduates at the 103 Bureau of Prison Institutions. Ms. Hill was just across the street and still part of the Forrest City Correctional Compound, but it seemed like she was a million miles away.

The job in education got more difficult as new teachers took over the GED classroom. The testing wasn't as consistent, and as a result, fewer men were passing the real test. Some instructors just wanted to make sure the men were in the classroom but didn't seem to care much if they were successful or not. It became more and more difficult for the volunteers that came in and for the tutors.

The softball season started in March, but the umpire/scorekeeping classes I taught started in February. My unit team won the league championship and the tournament championship. That league ended in late June. I made the all-star team and pitched the all-star game, which we also won. I led the league in batting average. The draft league started in July and ran through mid-October. My team won the league and tournament championships there too. Again, I led the league in batting average.

Our White Boy Team was the best softball team that ever came through Forrest City Complex. We began to really dominate the Tuesday/Wednesday pickup games. In the October on a Tuesday afternoon, we were finishing up a game around dusk. I began to notice I was having trouble seeing the ball when it was thrown to me. Occasionally the ball, when it was hit, I had no idea where it went. That was dangerous situation since I was only forty-six inches away from the batter, and the batter often crushed the softball. We had to stop the game because I couldn't see. Reading also became more difficult.

I finally got in to see the eye doctor in medical. I hoped to get some new glasses. Much to my surprise, he told me I had cataracts. He said my eyes were as bad as seventy-five-year-old man might have. I was only fifty-two years old. By Christmas, my vision was 20/400 in both eyes. I was legally blind.

I couldn't play softball in 2004 because I could not see the ball. In July of 2004, I was sent out to have my lenses measured in both eyes for lens replacement surgery. I would spend the next sixteen months legally blind and waiting on a promised surgery that seemed to be only a promise. I was running into men on the sidewalk because I literally could not see them. My world had grown considerable darker. My life seemed more suspended than ever. Everything I did was affected by this blinder. There was only one significant event that year that really shook my world and left me feeling more desperate and separated than ever before.

Chapter 42

(Carey)

It was mid-August 2004 and hot. I had gone to bed on a Sunday night and slept pretty well. At about 3:00 a.m. early Monday morning, the same female lieutenant that had awakened me in the middle of the night when Mom passed away was in my cube again.

"Wake up, Phillips. Phillips, get up," she said.

I sat up in bed and saw her standing there. Last time Mom had died. Her presence sent a chill down my spine.

I said, "What's wrong?"

She said, "Just get up, Phillips. I'll wait for you outside on the porch."

I already had my sweatpants on, so I slipped on my tennis shoes, walked to the door, and stepped out on the porch. I followed her down the two flights of stairs. I was wide awake. As we started across the compound, I said, "Who is it, Lieutenant? Is it my son?"

I don't know why I thought it was about him. He was twenty-eight and worked at the casino. She looked at me and said, "'Yes, Jack. It is your son." There was real empathy in her voice and in her eyes.

I could only ask, "Is he dead?"

She stopped and looked at me and said. "Jack, I honestly don't know. Let's get to the office, and you can call home and find out all you want to know. I am sorry." When she apologized, I immediately thought he was dead. He must have been in a car wreck.

She took me into the back office (where I had been taken when Mom died) and said, "Call your brother." She slid the phone across the desk. I called Paul's cell phone, and he answered on the second ring.

As soon as he answered, I asked, "Is he dead? Is he alive?" I was thinking car accident, but I was wrong about that.

Paul said, "Jack, he is in surgery. Carey was shot, Jack. He was shot in the knee with a shotgun at point-blank range. He was then beaten over his head with the butt of the shotgun and left for dead. He has lost a lot of blood."

I was stunned and sick. All I could say was, "Paul, is he going to make it? Is he going to live?"

Paul calmly said, "They think so. Jack, he might lose his left leg."

I pictured all the times I had watched him run so gracefully and athletically since he was a child. It hurt to think my only son was battling for his life and battling to keep his leg, and once again I was living a suspended life and unable to even go to the hospital to see him. I needed to be with my only son. I knew Paul and Mary Lynn would be there, but Kara and I should be there too. Neither one could do anything for our son except pray often and harder than we ever had before. Honestly, I didn't think I could take it if he died (or even if he lost his leg).

I asked Paul, "Who did this to him?"

Paul told me, "A guy he worked with. It had to do with Jessie [that was Carey's fiancé]. We don't know much, but apparently it revolved around her. Carey had ridden to Missouri with Mary Lynn to pick up Mary Lynn's oldest two children, who had spent the weekend with their father in Missouri. When Mary Lynn let Carey out at his house about midnight, Carey said something about it being odd that Jessie wasn't home. He must have been shot at that other guy's place or somewhere in between. That's about all we know." I told Paul I would call him at 6:00 a.m., as soon as the phones in the unit came on.

The lieutenant sent me back to my unit. It was 4:10 a.m. I just paced the unit until the lights/phones came on at 6:00 a.m. About all I found out on the first call was that he was out of surgery and the doctors thought he would live. Carey would be in the hospital for four months. He didn't lose the leg (although he had the option to have it removed). Instead, they put a metal rod from his thigh to his ankle. They just removed his knee. His leg would be about two inches shorter than the other one and stiff the rest of his life. Carey would never run again.

The man that shot him on purpose was never prosecuted. However, that man would die from cancer four years later at age thirty-four. I really understood for the first time how much God the Father had loved us to sacrifice his only Son.

My spiritual life was changing, and as a result, my life was changing in every respect. This suspended life didn't look quite as bad as before. God had answered our prayer and saved our son. I would see him and hear him and hug him and laugh with him again.

Chapter 43

More of the Same

In 2004, Chaplain Crosby was transferred to the medium high. The chaplain department was not immune to interoffice squabbling. First, Ms. Hill had left in education, and now Chaplain Crosby. The two staff members that meant the most to me were now gone. I missed them both more than I could have imagined. My son, Carey, had recovered and was now trying to piece together a life for himself. I was still blind.

Keith Hawkins had served his time (seventy months) and been released in 2003. We communicated by letter as best we could since our contact was actually in violation of his probation and not allowed at my institution. He also checked with Paul to see how I was doing and if I needed anything. He was furious that medical had let me run around blind for sixteen months without acting. Keith told me not to worry. He said he would figure out a way to get my eyes fixed.

I was at work in education one day around 2:00 p.m. when an announcement came over the speaker for me to report to my unit manager immediately. I was released from education and went back to the unit and in the inner hallway to the unit manager's office. I knocked on the door, and she said, "Come in, Phillips." I went in, and she motioned for me to take a chair in front of her desk. I had no idea why she had called me in.

She laid down her pen, looked at me, and said, "Mr. Phillips, can I ask you something?"

I said, "Sure."

She asked, "Jack, who do you know in the White House?"

I said, "The White House? The White House where the president lives?"

She said, "Yes," and slid a letter across the desk. I could tell it was expensive stationery. I quickly read the letter. In summary, it said, "Why is Mr. Phillips walking around blind? Why has Mr. Phillips been blind for over a year and not received the proper medical treatment? Why has Mr. Phillips not received the eye surgery he obviously needs? Please send a copy of Mr. Phillip's medical records to my office, the office of the president of the United States, as soon as possible." The letter had the presidential seal embossed on the letter and was signed, "The Office of the President of the United States." I slid the letter back across the desk to her. I was just as shocked as she was. I had no idea it was coming.

She asked again "So, Jack, who do you know in the White House?"

I said to her, "I can't tell you that. I can't divulge my contact there." (Actually, I knew no one even close to the White House, but she didn't know that.)

She slid more papers at me along with a pen and then said, "You need to read these and sign them so we can release your medical records. They need to be mailed out this afternoon."

I read the papers, signed them, and left. As I was leaving the unit and heading back across the compound to education, I heard another announcement. This announcement informed me I needed to report to medical immediately. I changed directions and headed over to medical.

When I arrived, I was immediately directed down the hall to the supervisor of medical office. His name was Mr. Ramirez. He was a nervous small man. I knocked on his door, and he told me to come in. I had never seen him so shaken. He asked me to please take a chair. He told me he too had received a letter from the office of the president of the United States. He informed me they wanted my medical records and I needed to sign so they could release them. His hands were literally shaking.

He pulled out a yellow legal pad after all the signing, looked at me, and said, "Mr. Phillips, I want to apologize on behalf of medical and the facility here for not providing your treatment for your eyes in a timely manner. The reason that happened is that your file apparently was placed in the wrong stack, and we lost track of your records. However, I am going to write out a contract with you today. This will guarantee you will have your eye surgery in three to ten days. I can't say which day because of security reasons, but be assured it has already been scheduled."

With that, he began to write on the yellow legal pad. He slid the pad across for me to read. I told him, "Just add at the top the date and the time." I slid it back, and he did.

I then added, "While you are at it, call the nurse here with the most longevity and have her sign it as a witness."

He said, "Oh, sure." He called on the phone for the nurse. She came in and signed the document as a witness. I had her put the time and date by her signature too.

He informed me he would have the nurse make a copy and give it to me. I told him that would not do. I told him to have the nurse make a copy (or two) for their files and one for the president to send along with my medical records, and I would keep the original document myself.

He was glad to accommodate me. I was calling the shots, and he knew it. He was petrified by that letter. It sure felt good to finally be in control of something affecting my life to such a great degree. The nurse left with the document and then returned the copies to him and the original to me.

Three days later I was in West Memphis, Arkansas, and had cataract surgery on my left eye. I could see great out of that eye. The surgery was a complete success. The eye doctor gave me a card to keep with the measurement of my right lens on it, and he said, "I'll see you again in a couple of weeks for that surgery." Little did I know that that would not happen for three more years.

Keith just laughed. He said he had written letters, sent faxes, and called over and over to finally get someone in the White House to talk to him. He told them they had put Michael Vick in prison for mistreating dogs but left me in the BOP to be treated worse than any dog. Thank God for Keith. I could now see (at least with one eye). That meant I could read again and play ball, even if it was with only one eye.

Chapter 44

Restored in 2005

I definitely reached a milestone and a change in direction when I could finally see again. Sixteen months or so in blindness had had an impact on me. I could now teach school and see, this time using the new methods I had developed while blind. It made me a much more effective teacher. I could also resume playing softball not only on my unit and draft teams but more importantly with the White Boy Team. Lastly, I could again conduct my Bible studies on my own, and my study and preparation improved significantly as did my personal spiritual life.

I had really missed softball. Being able to see and play again was a definite plus to my quality of life. Softball lasted ten months and was a big deal to the two thousand or so inmates at the low facility. I did have a little trouble because the depth perception with my new lens was not the same as before, and after all, I was still blind in one eye. However, I was still accomplished, and my teams competed for the championships, and the White Boy team just kept winning.

At school, I began to implement the different ways I had discovered to teach writing skill and English grammar. They worked like a charm, and I continued to perfect those as the days and weeks passed by. I was a much-better GED teacher than I had been before the blindness. Although the leadership in the department continued to decline, the teaching and work was much improved. I felt that I was in my element, and it was a great way to occupy my time and keep my mind off my imprisonment.

Spiritually, my life had made a dramatic change. I could not pinpoint the exact time or date that happened, but I know I began to see things through spiritual eyes. My joy and peace multiplied. I was coming out of the funk I had been in since Mom and Dad had died and Carey had been shot. I retyped the seven-thousand-page Bible study I had written and typed back in 2001–2003. I made it more student friendly by providing blanks that could be filled in by the students as we went through the study. It became more inter-active. I became a better teacher. I was much more sure of myself in biblical and spiritual matters. I was able to answer the myriad of questions that came my way both doctrinally and denominationally. Brother John Henson began visiting me once a month. He rode with Paul, and he was a great blessing to my personal spiritual life and to the Bible-study teaching. In addition, I was still serving on the ministerial team, which meant I was the worship leader with one of the chaplains about every nine or ten weeks. I still missed Chaplain Crosby, but I was comfortable working with some of the other chap-lains and even went through special training classes on witnessing and other Christian ministry work.

The violence increased significantly at the end of 2005 into 2006. The older white men leaders had gradually left the prison, and the white gang, the Dirty White Boys, took on a more prominent role on the compound. We had a drastic increase in the number of child pornographers; men were being convicted and sent to prison for downloading child porno on their personal computers. They were coming to prison in droves. There were still the occasional child molester showing up as well. They began to number in the hundreds just on our compound.

The Dirty White Boys began threatening those men with vio-lence if they didn't get off the compound (meant checking into pro-tective custody). Some checked in, and some didn't. If they failed to check in, sometime during a night, a pack of disguised gang mem-bers ran up in their cubes and beat them with locks. Often, they dragged these men who had been sleeping off their bunks face-first onto a metal table. They weren't just beaten with locks—they were beaten with fists and kicked repeatedly with steel-toed boots. It was violent, bloody, and even deadly. Most of the beaten men were taken to the hospital and never returned to our compound. I don't know if they died, were transferred, or remained hospitalized for extended periods. We just never saw them again. The perpetrators were rarely apprehended. It became a regular thing. Sadly, often after the fact, it was discovered they had gone into the wrong cube or, more likely, beaten a man that was not actually a child offender. It was cruel and violent and senseless. It would continue as long as I was at that low facility.

Chapter 45

Kara's Transfer

In 2006, Kara's transfer went through. She and another female inmate along with two prison guards and a pilot were flown on a small eight-seat plane to St. Louis, Missouri. From there, Kara and the other inmate were bussed to the Greenville, Illinois, Federal Bureau of Prisons Camp for Women. There was also a medium men's facility at the complex.

The camp had previously been a men's camp, but it had been converted to be a female camp because of the large increase in the number of women in the federal system. Kara would now be much closer to her family in Rector, Arkansas. She looked forward to seeing her family and having more visits from them and from our children, grandchildren, and Paul.

Kara was accepted into their dog-training program. They had a program to train adopted dogs to help the blind and the disabled. Kara loved dogs and was excited to be accepted. She was assigned a black lab puppy named Jeep, and she worked with Jeep during the day (as a job) and kept him in her room in a small pet kennel at night. The female inmates in the dog program lived in their own special section and were appreciated and recognized for the good work they did.

Kara was just settling in the first few weeks when she was notified that her oldest brother had passed away. He had lived at the family home with her mother and younger brother for a number of years. He had suffered a heart attack previously and had some health issues, but his death was unexpected. Kara was, of course, devastated. She had transferred to be closer to home hoping to see her family, including her oldest brother. It had happened so suddenly, and she had been there such a short period of time that it drained the joy out of her transfer. She hadn't been there long enough to ask and set up a trip for his funeral, so she had to deal with missing his funeral as well.

That was just the beginning. Kara was diabetic and had a few other medical ailments. Her first trip to medical resulted in a lab test. The results would not be good news. Shortly after the lab visit, she was on callout to go back to medical. She was diagnosed with muscular dystrophy. Her oldest brother had just died from the disease and the problems related to it. Kara was frightened by the diagnosis. She was also removed from the dog-training program because of its demands of constantly kneeling down and standing up in the training of the dogs. Although she still lived in the dog-training area and saw Jeep every day, she was not allowed to train him and could not keep a dog in her room. Seeing Jeep every day helped, but again she was very disappointed.

About five months later she was notified her younger brother had also died of muscular dystrophy at the family home. She and her brother were only ten months apart. He was fifty-three. She also knew her older sister (the only one surviving) had the disease, as did her son, Kara's nephew. She was able to attend her younger brother's funeral, which helped, but they were very close and had grown up as playmates. She was able to spend time with her family and friends as she attended the funeral, and her counselor and escort allowed her to go the family home for an hour or so after the funeral. That helped a lot. I hated that I had to miss the services for her brothers since I had known them both very well my whole life.

Kara's troubles weren't over. Two months later her mother passed away. Now, in one year, two of her brothers and her mom had passed away. Her hope to move to Illinois to have more visits and see her family had not panned out. It had been one disappointment after another. I wondered how much she could stand. Three deaths and removed from the dog program. She was now working in the kitchen at the facility, and her family had been nearly wiped out. She was regretting her transfer. She had had nothing but grief since she arrived in Illinois.

We had grown used to talking for ten to fifteen minutes on the phone on our anniversary and around Christmas for the last five years. Those phone calls and the two I made when Dad and then Mom died had been our only opportunities to talk on the phone. The staff at Greenville did not allow the women (even wives) to have phone calls with any other inmates (even their husbands). I called her mom's house about an hour after her mom's funeral, and her counselor/escort allowed us to talk on the phone. It had been almost a year. Little did I know I wouldn't talk to Kara again for four years. Not hearing each other's voice was painful and ridiculous. Our calls were all recorded and monitored. It was allowed but left up to the discretion of the warden at each particular institution. Just like the warden at FCI Memphis, her warden would not allow her to speak to me on the phone.

Our families were so intertwined after all the time we had been together that those loses affected me almost as severely as they affected her. I was also concerned about Kara working in the kitchen. I had done that on two different occasions and had been treated horribly both times. She worked in the kitchen there for the next four years. She didn't make much money on that job, so Aunt Jean, Paul, and Kara's brothers kept sending her the money she needed.

She did get a few more visits from Carey and Mary Lynn and the kids and Paul. That helped a lot, but by this point, it was so painful for Kara when they all left that she was content with no visits. I continued to write her a letter every day. The more depressed and alone she became, the fewer letters I received from her. I missed hearing from her. I wanted to reach out. I don't think I had ever been so lonely for her.

Chapter 46

Healthy

As Kara struggled with her depression and health, I had never been healthier. The fact that I only had one eye (still blind in my right eye) adversely affected my softball, but my overall health had never been better.

I started doing push-ups and running/walking in 2005, and all through 2006 and 2007, I continued. I was doing five hundred push-ups every day. I mixed up the number of push-ups and number of reps to avoid getting bored with the workout, but at least once a week I did five sets of one hundred each. I was proud, and my body began to show it. In addition, I was consistently running five miles a day.

My body had really changed. I was noticeably larger through my chest, upper arms, forearms, and back from all the push-ups. The running had toned my legs. There were well defined muscles all over me, and my weight had gone from about one hundred ninety pounds to two hundred ten pounds. My waist size had actually diminished about two inches. I looked like I weighed about one hundred eighty, but the two hundred and ten pounds was all good weight. I had several men that had observed the transformation ask me if I was taking steroids. I wasn't. I was just working consistently hard.

Kara on the other hand was restricted in her physical activities because of the muscular dystrophy. She was also depressed and bored. She began having blood pressure problems and cholesterol problems along with diabetes and thyroid problems. All that meant more medication. Put together, it left her listless with little desire to do much physically. The job in the kitchen required long hours, and that tired her out as well. We were never without something to worry about. Her health was the newest thing.

Chapter 47

Working on My Transfer

I had a team meeting with my unit team staff in April of 2007. I pointed out to them that in August, just four months away, I would be eligible to transfer to a camp because I would be under ten years. I reminded them my projected release date with good time was August 11, 2017. My next team meeting (unless it was a meeting to inform me of my transfer) would not occur until October 2007. I asked them to prepare my paperwork so I could leave as soon as my ten years remaining date arrived.

I also reminded them I had served almost nine years and had positive work reports and no discipline referrals. I had taken all the ACE (Adult Continuing Education) classes they had to offer and had completed a thirty-hour college program through the local community college and maintained a perfect 4.0 grade point average for the ten college classes. I had done my part. It was now time for them to do their part.

Kara was already at a camp, and her release to a halfway house would be coming up in a few years. It wasn't that I was just so anxious to go to a camp. I had never been and didn't even know if I would like it. I did remember what Mr. Green had told me at FCI Memphis back in 1999. "Son, if they want to send you to a lower-classification facility, you pack your bags and go willingly. It just means you are getting closer to the door and your time will be easier to do." I knew I wanted to be in a camp by the time Kara was out and at the halfway house because I knew she would finish that and possibly be able to come visit. I figured it would be easier for her to come visit me at a camp than at the low facility. They assured me they knew I was deserving of the camp and that they would do their part.

In July, I put a cop-out in to see my counselor, Mr. Barnes. He was a nice-looking black man that had a real estate job on the side in Memphis and was a huge football fan. His son was playing college football at one of the midmajor schools in Arkansas. He knew I had been a football coach, and he liked talking football with me. He told me in regard to the cop-out I submitted that he was working on my camp transfer papers and would call me in shortly after August 11, 2007, to update me on the possibility of me being transferred to camp.

He kept his word and called me in to tell me I had been turned down by Ms. Henderson. She was in administration, and all transfers had to be approved by her office. Ms. Pierce was the overall boss of that part of administration, but she allowed Ms. Henderson the power to approve or disapprove of such requests at the low and camp level. Ms. Pierce made the decisions at the medium facility. Mr. Barnes said he had no idea why Ms. Henderson denied the request.

I had my team meeting in October and again raised the issue of my camp transfer. My unit manager, Ms. Ruby-Smith, was in charge at the team meeting. She assured me that Mr. Barnes had, in fact, submitted my transfer papers and that Ms. Henderson had denied them. She convinced me they would have to wait six months to resubmit them again because Ms. Henderson had instituted a rule that transfer paperwork could only be submitted every six months. It wasn't BOP policy, but it was Ms. Henderson's rule. I also noticed my security level had not been lowered as it should have been. It was still at "Greatest." I never understood why it was that high anyway or how I was allowed to go to camp if that were true. It had been "Moderate" when I started out, and I had done nothing to change that.

Sometime in the winter of 2007, I ran into Ms. Pierce. Like Ms. Henderson, her office was not at the low. Her office was at the camp, so we rarely actually saw her at the low. She was equally powerful to an assistant warden. She was a beautiful middle-aged woman who treated the inmates like they were real people and not just things.

She treated us as if we had value and dignity and that our concerns really mattered to her. I told her about my concerns and the fact that Ms. Ruby-Smith seemed to have increased my security level from "Moderate" to "Greatest." She assured me she would look into my security level concerns and my camp transfer request. I was hesitant to mention Ms. Ruby-Smith because it was well-known she was Ms. Pierce's closest friend. I didn't want to criticize her too much. Ms. Pierce pointed out to me the problem might be overcrowding at the nearby camps.

I hadn't considered that. I really wanted to transfer to Millington (a suburb of Memphis) because it was only about fifteen minutes from Paul's house. He continued to come visit every Saturday. It was over a one-hundred-mile drive for him to come to Forrest City and home each Saturday. I also knew Kara would be living at his house when she was released. With her living with Paul and Jen, it would make sense for me to go to Millington. Kara would have five years of supervised release whenever she was released from BOP custody. With her probation officer's permission, she could come visit. Permission was much more likely to be given if I was in the same state and even in the same county.

I wasn't panicked about the lack of transfer, at least not yet, and I was trying not to be angry at how the entire matter was being handled, but even that was consistent with how other issues were handled in the BOP. Incompetence and lack of concern seemed to rule every day and every situation. Kara hadn't received her halfway house date yet, so it wasn't time for me to panic.

Chapter 48

Early 2008

I had sent Keith Hawkins, my friend and former cellmate, a Christmas card in December 2007. He had been out almost four years, but he was struggling to find a decent job and get back on his feet. I received a letter back from him in early January 2008. In that letter, he asked me if I had ever had the surgery on my right eye. He said if they still had not done the surgery to let him know and he would get on it. I smiled thinking about the letter from the office of the president that had resulted in the surgery on my left eye in 2005. I wrote him back and told him they continued to deny me the surgery and actually told me no one ever gets surgery on both eyes and all a person really needs is one eye! I didn't know if he could pull another rabbit out of the hat and help me again or not.

Kara had a team meeting in February 2008. She called Paul at home and then wrote me a letter telling us all that she would be released to the halfway house in Memphis (for a six-month stay) in April of 2010. Even though it was still two years away, she could see the light at the end of the tunnel, and it wasn't an oncoming train!

I immediately asked my counselor to file my camp papers again. He said he would. After a week or ten days, he called me in and said for some reason Ms. Henderson had denied me again. He even told me, "Phillips, maybe Ms. Henderson just doesn't like you." I told him Ms. Henderson didn't even know me. Although I still had two years until Kara would be released and I could afford to wait patiently for now, I began to really grow concerned. Paul was not getting any younger, and the plus-one-hundred-mile trip seemed to be taking its toll. It was a real wear and tear on him and his car. I kept having a nagging thought that they might never let me go to the camp. I didn't know why! That's what was really nagging at me.

Chapter 49

Changing Times

In April 2008, I went to team meeting and again broached the issue of a camp transfer. They gave me the "wait six months and we will see" speech again. I was getting upset because I was never given a why for the denials. I wouldn't have another team meeting until October 2008.

Out of the blue, I was called to medical one day (I think it was late March or early April) and asked to sign another release for them to release my medical records so they could send them to the office of the president of the United States. Keith had struck again! Two days later I was in West Memphis, Arkansas, having lens replacement surgery on my right eye. It had been five years since I could see out of both eyes. Thank God! The optometrist that came in, the same one who told me five years earlier they "only do one eye," said he had worked as a contractor with the feds at the prison for seventeen years and had never seen anyone have surgery on both eyes for any reason. Keith had overcome all the odds, and now I could see.

I couldn't wait to play softball. My unit and draft teams breezed through championships. The White Boy Team had turned over personnel, but we just kept winning. From 2006–2008, the White Boy Team went 97–3. We played all comers. Put a team together of anyone you want, and we will play you. I hit .787 and was intentionally walked when I came to bat with men on base and the game on the line. That was a great compliment to a player my age. I turned fifty-seven that summer.

It wasn't all fun and games. I began having severe arthritis pain in my wrist, hands, elbows, and shoulders. I was eating eight-hundred-milligram Tylenol and Motrin like they were candy just to be able to play. The pain was excruciating. Without the large doses of the anti-inflammatory drugs, I couldn't lift my arms above my shoulders or even grip a bat. I was having trouble sleeping and writing on the whiteboard at school and quickly went from doing five hundred push-ups a day to not being able to do more than one.

Even worse, lab results showed I had suffered significant damage to my kidneys and possibly liver by taking all the Tylenol and Motrin. I was taken multiple times to the hospital in Memphis, where they did a sonar on my kidneys. They took over one hundred thirty-six vials of blood that year. I never saw the reports or the results of my hospital visits.

Chapter 50

My Transfer Finalized

I still hadn't seen Ms. Henderson. She had an office at the medium facility, and I couldn't get there from the low. I prepared a cop-out along with seven pages of prison policy regarding camp transfer and took it in to Mr. Barnes along with a letter I had typed for him to give to Ms. Henderson. What he didn't know was that I prepared the exact cop-out with the copies of the policy, and after he got his copy, I dropped hers in the unit mailbox. This was still several weeks before my next team meeting. I had now been eligible for the camp for fourteen months! Kara's release date of April 10, 2010, was getting closer and closer, and I was losing my patience with them.

About a week after dropping off the papers to Mr. Barnes and sending Ms. Henderson a copy through the mail, Mr. Barnes called me to his office over the intercom. It was about 3:30 p.m. I reported to his office, and he handed me my cop-out. He said, "Jack, I am so sorry, but Ms. Henderson denied you again."

I was devastated. I looked at the bottom half of the first page of the cop-out, and he had written, "I am sorry, Mr. Phillip. Ms. Henderson has declined your request again. We all think you should be at the camp. We have no idea why Ms. Henderson keeps denying you."

I asked him, "Did you give her the personal two-page letter I had typed her?"

He said, "Yes, I did. Well, I didn't really give it to her, but I did read it to her over the phone."

I left his office and returned to my cube for the four-o'clock count. When the count cleared, we had mail call [as we always did after four-o'clock count]. My name was called, and I was surprised to find the answer to my cop-out I had sent Ms. Henderson. Finally, a real response from her! I hoped I would now find out why she was denying me a transfer to camp. I returned to my cube, removed the staple that held it all together, and began to read her response written on the bottom half of the front page of my cop-out It said, "Mr. Phillips, I have examined your record and believe you should already be at the camp. You are an ideal candidate for the camp. Just ask your unit team to submit your paperwork, and I will certainly approve it."

What? It hit me like a ton of bricks. Ms. Henderson, whom I blamed for denying my camp transfer requests for fourteen months, had never even seen my camp request paperwork. Mr. Barnes and Ms. Ruby-Smith had both been lying to me the entire time. My boss in education had looked up the camp at Millington and the one at Forrest City. There was plenty of space at both.

I jumped up and went back to Mr. Barnes in his office. I laid the cop-out he had written me on his desk and then showed him the one that Ms. Henderson had written (dated the same day as his). He reached to take it out of my hands, but I pulled it back. I told him, "No, you don't! You don't get this one. One of you has lied to me. I now have it in your own handwritings. You don't get this one. This is my proof that someone has lied. Why have you been lying to me about this? Also, you never read that letter to Ms. Barnes. It would take you fifteen or twenty minutes to read it to her. She would have told you to fax it to her or scan it on your computer. You lied about that too?"

He wouldn't look at me. I told him, "You know, I haven't been real concerned about the camp because my wife won't be out until April 2010. However, I don't like being lied to and treated like I don't matter or, worse, like I am stupid. I now have two federal documents. Someone has committed fraud on a federal document. That is a felony. I will pursue this and get to the bottom of it. Someone is going to lose his or her job over this. I hope they end up in prison just like me."

He couldn't say a word. If a black man could look pale, then he had paled right in front of me. I now had something to work with. I was only a few days away from my team meeting. I had to figure out my strategy.

The next day I took the papers to work with me and made additional copies. I was afraid they would search my locker and simply remove the evidence and deny it had ever existed. On my way to lunch, I ran into Ms. Pierce. Boy, was I glad to see her! I gave her a rundown and showed her the paperwork. She was just shaking her head. As she finished reading, Ms. Ruby-Smith walked up.

Ms. Pierce smiled and said, "Hi, June! Did you change Mr. Phillips's custody to low like I told you to?"

She looked at me and said, "I called region, and your custody should never have been 'Greatest.'" She looked back at Ms. Ruby-Smith, and she said, "Yes, I did."

Ms. Pierce smiled at her friend and said, "Thank you."

She turned to me and said, "Jack, you are going to the camp. I took care of that myself in talking with region yesterday." It was amazing. While I was dealing with Mr. Barnes and Ms. Henderson, Ms. Pierce was looking out for me. She was certainly a very special person.

Two days later I went to team meeting. I was informed I needed to pack because I would be going to the camp the next day. They indicated I would be going across the street to the camp in Forrest City and not to Millington.

I saw Ms. Pierce the next morning on my way to work. I had a feeling she was looking for me. She said, "Jack, I know they told you you were going across the street, and I also know you wanted to go to Millington. Don't give up on Millington. I called region again to see if they could move you to Millington if possible. I don't know if I was too late or if it will happen." I thanked her for all she had done.

The same day at three o'clock, I was called to R and D. That meant I was going right then. I found out I would not be going to Millington. I packed my belongings went through R and D, loaded on a van, and was driven just down and across the street to the camp at Forrest City.

As I was going through R and D, I was talking to an officer I had now known for eight years. He was excited for me to be leaving for the camp and assured me it was better. I told him I could have been there in August of 2007, but I had been delayed, although I had no reason why.

He looked at me and said, "Jack, you know why, don't you?"

I was startled that he said that, but I replied, "Yeah, I guess I offended Mr. Barnes or Ms. Ruby-Smith."

He said, "No, it goes higher than that. Remember a few years back when you wrote the letter for your counselor, Mr. Gill? Remember the judge sentenced him according to your recommendation and not according to the ex-warden's recommendation?"

I said, "Yeah, I remember."

He said, "You embarrassed them and pissed them off. They have been punishing you for getting involved in institution business. That's how they rot in here."

I told him if they had told me I wasn't going to the camp for trying to help Mr. Gill, I could have handled that I would have withdrawn my request to go to the camp. The letter I wrote to the judge for Mr. Gill was the right thing to do. I was proud of it regardless the cost.

I think one of the hardest parts of leaving the low was leaving my cellmate of six and a half years. Joe Hunter was my friend. More like a brother. When an inmate lives with someone that long, strong bonds develop. Sure, we got on each other's nerves from time to time, but we had become dependable and reliable best friends. We had even worked together for a while. He was due to be at the camp shortly, so I knew he would probably come across the street just as I had. I knew I would miss him, and I did every day. I had been at the low for eight years and six months. I was ready for a change, and I knew I was one step closer to the door, just as Mr. Green had told me.

Chapter 51

Illness and Chaplain Crosby

I was sick. When I arrived at the camp, many of the men who had known me from the low didn't recognize me shuffling down the sidewalk all bent over and hurting. There were weeks at a time I could barely get out of bed. I went to medical and tried to get medical attention, but my appointments were made four to six weeks later. Way too late to help me. The arthritis was killing me. I had to tie my arm to the bedpost at night in an upward angle just to relieve the pain so I could fall asleep. Of course, every time I moved, I woke up. I was pale as a ghost, and I believed I was suffering from both kidney and liver damage from the anti-inflammatory drugs I had taken. During the winter of 2008 and 2009, it was all I could do to walk to the chow hall, to school, and to church, and all three were just a short walk away.

Eventually, they put me on stronger pain medicine (only five milligrams at a time) and another medication for gout. Over time that medication helped, but in the meantime I often felt my death was imminent, even to the point I didn't care. I tried to play softball in 2009, but I was only able to play about half the games. That would be my last season to play softball. After that I served as the commissioner of the softball league(s). That paid me twenty-five dollars a month for ten months out of the year. That helped me get by with my education money.

In education, I was reunited with Ms. Gill and loved every minute of working with her. There was never a dull moment when she was around. In addition, in August of 2009, computers were installed in the library, and inmates were allowed to use the TRULINCS system, which allowed us to e-mail family and friends at a minimal cost. I was even allowed to e-mail Kara from institution to institution after we both obtained permission. Our e-mails were usually delivered within a couple of hours. It really sped up our ability to communicate. I continued to write her letters daily, but she quit writing letters in favor of e-mailing. I was paid fifty-five dollars a month as the TRULINCS guy; all the extra money meant I didn't have to be dependent on any money from the family. However, Aunt Jean continued to send Kara and I fifty dollars a month anyway.

By the first week of October 2008, Chaplain Crosby had been transferred from the medium back to the low. That meant he would also be in charge of the camp. I was so glad to be back under his ministry because he was a lot more to me than just a chaplain. He was a great friend and mentor. By the first week of November, I was teaching the Bible-study camp-wide on Wednesday nights. We had an inmate pastor of the church at the camp that did a wonderful job. There were about six inmates that rotated preaching on Sunday nights. I was added to that list in November 2008. In December, he appointed me assistant pastor and notified me that he would be leaving and going home in 2009, and he wanted me to take over the church as pastor. I officially took that title on July 21, 2009. We had volunteers that came in on Sunday morning and another on Monday nights. Sometimes Chaplain Crosby or other chaplains showed up on Sunday morning and did the services.

One by one the volunteers stopped coming, and one by one the inmates preaching went home or were transferred. It wasn't too long before I was doing the Sunday morning service, the Sunday evening service, and the Monday evening service and teaching the Bible study on Wednesday nights. Pastors that had been convicted came to the camp, and we helped train and develop men that felt like God was calling them in to the ministry. They all did a great job, and God blessed our church.

Because of my position as pastor of the church, I was held to a higher standard of behavior on the compound. I lived up to that standard. I was accountable to God, to the chaplains, to the inmate church members, to the staff, and to all the inmates on the compound. As a result, the level of trust shown in me and to me by the chaplains, the staff, and the inmates soared. I was able to counsel with all the above when various trials and tribulations came their way.

There were a few real shockers for me at the camp. First, there were toilet seats on all the commodes. I had not sat on a toilet seat in ten years. Toilet seats could be ripped off and used as weapons, so they were not available at the medium or low facility. When I saw the toilet seats on all the commodes, I felt like I was at a resort. It is a shame that something so common could mean so much. Secondly, the front door to my unit was never locked! It remained open twenty-four hours a day. We were in an honor situation, and the open door said to me, "You are on your honor not to abuse this." Unfortunately, not every inmate felt that way.

There was no fence around the camp. It fact, it was surrounded by farmland and crops—cotton, beans, etc. Inmates at the camp had proven trustworthy. Being at the camp was a privilege an inmate had earned. However, there was a constant movement late at night of inmates running across the fields, as we called it. Sometimes they left and had women pick them up across the fields or even on the turn rows of the fields. Others just went to pick up large duffel bags that had been left in the fields that brought in tremendous amounts of contraband. Cell phones were outlawed, but their presence allowed safer crossing of the fields since an inmate could be warned if it was dangerous to come in and if it was safe. Cell phones were plentiful as were drugs, cigarettes, alcohol, food, and everything else you can imagine. When the staff had shakedowns and found contraband, it usually resulted in group discipline. That is, they took our televisions or suspended some other privilege, like the microwaves or visits, to punish us. It created a lot of bad feelings between inmates and staff and even caused problems within the inmate population. It could not nor would it ever solve the contraband problem.

Another pastime at the camp was stealing. Inmates at the camp worked in the warehouses that supplied the medium, the low, and the camp. They had access to food, clothing, lockers, metal shelves, and everything else. A book of stamps or books of stamps could buy you virtually anything you could get on the street. If you couldn't get it from the warehouse guys, you could always get it from the contraband guys. They stole so much food they couldn't eat it all. They cooked exotic dishes in the microwaves and even held fish fries and cooked fried chicken. They made homemade ice cream and other special dishes that were all for sale for x number of stamps. The entire unit often smelled like a gourmet restaurant. Unfortunately, as pastor of the church, I couldn't indulge in anything that had been stolen, including the food. I was watched to see if I practiced what I preached.

Inmates at the camp were also able to get institution driver's licenses. We were allowed to drive cars, vans, pickups, garbage trucks, four-wheelers, tractors, and forklifts. Some inmates were transport drivers and drove transferring inmates to Memphis or Little Rock and picked up other transferring inmates at those locations. The garbage trucks ran daily routes that covered a hundred miles or more. It was hard to believe I could go to the message center and get the keys to a brand-new minivan full of gas and drive off by myself. I wasn't supposed to leave the compound area, but I did have penalty to pay for such action. The cost was too steep for me. We did have men occasionally walk off from the camp. They recaptured most, but some men got completely away. If caught, they received extra years. I hadn't driven in ten years. It was quite a thrill to get behind the wheel again. It was like riding a bike—you never forget how to do it.

Chapter 52

School and More

The day I had arrived at the camp, Ms. Gill made me feel right at home in education. She had gotten word I was on my way, so she wasn't surprised to see me. She just squealed with delight when I walked up to her office door. She came running around the desk and hugged me really hard. She took me around the hallway to the classroom area. In the first classroom, I saw Ms. Pat Brady sitting behind the desk. Pat was a retired public elementary schoolteacher. She now worked for the local vo-tech school that volunteered her services to the prison to help teach the GED. She had already been there a number of years. I had met her more than once at the various in-service training sessions at the low. She was as happy to see me as Ms. Gill. She ran out of the room into the hallway and hugged me and shouted, "You' re finally here! Now take over!"

I grew to love Ms. Brady. We didn't always agree on things educationally, and I wasn't as big an Arkansas Razorback fan as her, but we certainly cared about and respected each other. Later I also worked with another volunteer (and retired high school history teacher) named Jerry Welker. We had much in common. Eventually, Ms. Brenda Wisdom, a volunteer I had known at the low and Ms. Brody's best friend, came to work at the camp as well. Ms. Wisdom was n retired high school English teacher that I had worked in the same department with at the low for about three years.

Not only were these three people valuable assets in the GED program, but they truly cared about the inmates, especially the inmate tutors. Ms. Brady made sure we had a microwave and coffee pot in our storage room for our use and theirs, and she also provided coffee and creamer and sugar (as did Ms. Gill) for our benefit. It was so nice to have freshly brewed coffee every day and was a big change for someone like me, who had been locked away for more than ten years.

We also ate well at the in-service training, which was held at the camp about six days a year. Staff members from the low and the medium also come to these meetings. I made presentations and showed them different teaching techniques and actually helped organize most of them.

At one of these in-service training sessions, I was asked to reveal to Ms. Franks my teaching techniques that I had developed when I was blind. She was from Little Rock and worked in the State Department of Education. Her job was to oversee all the GED programs in the state. She was the dog. After about twenty minutes, she pulled Ms. Gill and me into the highway. She asked me, "Mr. Phillips, how did you come up with all of this?"

I told her, "Believe it or not, I developed most of these techniques while I was blind."

She said, "I have been over the state GED program for twenty-seven years. I'm in and out of GED classrooms all over the state almost every day. I have just never seen anything like it!"

She turned around to Ms. Gill, who was standing there beaming, and said, "Can he leave the facility?"

Ms. Gill responded, "Yes, he is out custody and can leave as long as he is escorted. I could escort him myself."

Ms. Franks said, "I would like to have him conduct in-service training in all four sections of Arkansas starting in the northeast corner. If I can arrange that, can you do the rest here?"

Ms. Gill said, "We can do that!"

She told me to write up the new techniques and send her something so she would have something to use to justify organizing such large gatherings for in-service. I was thrilled. It was like being honored again for my teaching ability. I wrote it all up in a book on English grammar and writing the essay for the GED. The book was entitled *Teaching It Perfectly (TIP)*. Although this never developed because of serious health problems that afflicted Ms. Franks and forced her to retire, I would use the book for future in-service trainings when outside GED teachers were brought in for all-day training sessions using my material. We set up the visiting room for those special in-service training sessions and they were huge successes.

Later, I devised a new way to teach the math curriculum in the GED program by dividing the subject matter into three areas. It was written up in a booklet called *GED Math to the Third Power*. After the creation of this program, we broke the record for the number of GED graduates at the camp for three straight years. Every GED program in the country could benefit from these changes.

Before I left the camp, I was the guest speaker at six graduations. Later, I would be the guest speaker for the institution's volunteer banquets held annually to honor all the volunteers (about one hundred men and women) that worked at the three institutions, which made up the Forrest City Complex. No other inmate before or since has ever spoken to these groups. I was extremely honored to be asked to do that.

Chapter 53

The Church and Illness

I had been serving as the assistant pastor of the church since December of 2008. When our inmate pastor left on July 21, 2009, I became the inmate pastor of the church at the camp. It was at about that time we picked up the Monday night service. Within a year, I was doing three sermons and teaching the Bible study each week. It required a great effort to stay prepared. I had never prayed nor studied so hard.

During the fall of 2009, a great illness befell me. I barely had the strength to walk to the chapel. The podium held me up for many of the services I preached. I began suffering dry-eye and dry-mouth syndrome about the same time. This was not minor thing, so I made more trips to the Memphis hospital to see urologists and rheumatologists and other specialists, but there were never return trips like there were supposed to be. Finally, my strength seemed to return, but the dry eyes and dry mouth continued to plague me.

I discovered pasturing a church was difficult. This one had its own peculiar problems. I had so many different denominations, races, ethnic groups, and backgrounds in the church, everyone had his own idea of how things should go. My outward life had to appear impeccable in regard to behavior. I still struggled with bad thoughts about the justice system and some about the people that helped put Kara and me away. However, they were less hateful and less frequent. I was learning how to let the past be the past.

Brother John Henson, my childhood pastor and friend, continued to be my source for answers when church questions came up. The church began to dominate my daily life. I was still teaching school and still commissioner of softball and still the TRULINCS guy, but more and more of my thoughts and time were consumed by my duties as the inmate pastor of the church. I rarely had any downtime and seemed to be on the job seven days (and many nights) a week. I went to work at 5:30 a.m. and left at 8:30 p.m. each day seven days a week.

Thank God I had a television and VCR in my classroom. I stayed in that room all the time. Because I only had class for two hours a day, I had plenty of time for church preparation and time to watch the news and sports. I recorded shows and movies and watched them later. The television, like the microwave and coffee pot, was a real blessing. It was hardly like the prison time I had done before I came to the camp.

Chapter 54

(Kara)

Kara's time was passing quickly. April 2010 was just around the corner. We suffered through Thanksgiving and Christmas again away from the family. We spent those days with our fellow inmates. It was helpful for me to know that Kara would not miss another Thanksgiving or Christmas in prison. The last time we had both been home for Thanksgiving and Christmas had been 1997.

Every time holidays rolled around, it was painful. I taught hundreds of new inmates what I call the holiday principle. I had learned that it was much harder on our families at home on the special holidays than it was for us. We missed our families, but our absence was more pronounced at home on these special holidays. We were missed more on those days than any other times of the year. Our chair around the Thanksgiving table would be empty. The holiday principle was as follows: Never write, call, or e-mail and let the family know how much you are missing them on those days. The family will already miss you badly. Our purpose is to not make them miserable on their holiday. Our purpose is to not make things more difficult for them.

That meant when we called home, we had to be upbeat and positive. We would brag about how good our meals were and how much we enjoyed the day and all the special activities they had planned for us. We would encourage our families to enjoy the holidays and remind them we would be home soon and that everything was just fine with us. We had to do the same things in e-mails and letters.

Some inmates were able to get visits on those days. However, we always tried to tell the families they didn't have to come visit us. This seemed to take pressure off our families, and hopefully, that enabled them to enjoy the holidays more. It released them from any guilt they might feel for not visiting us. I think it was some of the best advice ever handed out.

Kara soared through the holiday season and began preparing boxes of her possessions to send home before she departed the facility in April. For the first time in decades, there was real joy in our family because of Kara's upcoming release. She was preparing as much as she could for *the* day.

Chapter 55

Kara's Release

As April grew closer, the excitement for the family continued to grow. It was decided that Paul and Jen would go in their car, Mary Ann and her husband and children could go in another car and Abel and his wife and Carey would go in a third car. She would have an entire host to welcome her when she came out of prison.

I reminded them to please take a camera and take as many photos as they could because I wanted to at least see photos to feel more a part of her release. Little did I know, I wouldn't actually get a copy of those photos until September. I was upset with that one since it had been my idea to take a camera.

What I was looking forward to was being able to call on one of their cell phones and be able to actually speak with Kara. Someone in each car had a cell phone, and I had all their numbers on my phone list. I planned on calling from the moment they picked her up and talking all the way to Memphis as they drove home from Greenville, Illinois. It would be roughly a six-hour trip. They had given her eight hours before she had to report to the halfway house in Memphis. We had not spoken on the phone in almost four years since we last talked, when her mom had passed away. I was so looking forward to actually hearing her voice again.

There was only one problem in my thinking: my phone situation. I only had three hundred minutes a month, but I would be able to save up my minutes for that day. The real problem was I could only talk fifteen minutes before my phone cut off. I then had to wait thirty minutes to call again. During the day, there was usually only one phone working and more than one hundred men in my unit. Many would want to use the phone that day. I was also going to have to take the day off at work, which I had not done in twelve years. It also meant having to hang around that phone and stand in line if necessary to call her as much as I could in the eight hours she had.

Ms. Gill was the one that insisted I take the day off. She even closed the school so that I wouldn't miss any classroom time. Out of respect for me and our situation, the men in the unit agreed to make sure when it was time form to call, the phone would be available. They postponed their calls for me to make mine! No one would stay on or get on the phone to mess up my fifteen minutes when that time rolled around. They made all their calls during my thirty-minute wait periods. I couldn't think of a more selfless thing anyone had ever done for me at any time. What an act of kindness! It was truly a warm and considerate gesture. Some men had set times to call their loved ones, and they sacrificed for me. They understood I had only talked to her about ten times in twelve years and not at all in almost four years. I was so appreciative and thanked and thanked all the men over and over in our unit. I even went around and left treats on the beds of everyone in the unit periodically for the rest of the time I was there. No one ever knew it was me leaving the treats. I left some on my bed so even my cellmate couldn't figure it out.

What joy I felt when I knew she was safely out! She had survived and had persevered. My respect for her was at an all-time high. They had not broken her. She had grown both emotionally and spiritually. Between calls that day, I found myself praising God for watching over her.

And those calls! To just hear her sweet voice touched my heart. I cried and laughed and laughed and cried. I heard her laughter and the sweet tone of her voice that I had enjoyed and valued for more than forty years.

I felt like half of me was traveling down I-55 headed to Memphis. Each time I called, they were closer. I talked to her for about one hundred minutes that day. I was feeling like I was with her all the way to the halfway house. I was so relieved she was actually out of prison.

It made my time easier because I didn't have the same worries that I had had. It also made me miss home more than ever. I could handle that though because I knew she was free. Yes, she was at the halfway house, but she was wearing her own clothes and wasn't in a prison uniform. Mary Lynn had fixed her up with everything she needed. There was joy in our family that had been missing for a long, long time.

Chapter 56

Funerals and Memorial Services

During the spring and summer of 2010, I had to deal with some new experiences as the inmate pastor of the camp church. We had a rash of deaths both in the inmate population and in the families of inmates that died.

Some of the men that died there at the camp were just found dead in their beds in their cube. Some others were victims of cancer and had been sent to federal prison medical units and died while they were there. Every inmate suffered when another inmate died. There was a consistent feeling of "there you go, I accept by the grace of God."

In many cases, deaths were the result of inadequate medical care. The medical care at the VA hospitals has been in the spotlight recently, but we experienced the same neglect in the BOP daily. Many of those men had recurring illnesses but never received the treatment they needed. It was simple negligence. In some cases, they we literally just left to die.

We had an older gentleman whose wife ultimately died of cancer. He had worked for Dick Cheney. When Cheney became Vice President, he replaced Chaney at Halliburton. He and his wife had homes in Singapore, London, Houston, and the family home in North Carolina. He was a very warm and intelligent man whom everyone respected. He requested to go see his wife when she was on her deathbed for about a three-week period. His approval came through about a month after she died. He tried to go to her funeral after she passed away. Our counselor, Mr. Racine, would have to escort him. It was approved, but he was going to have to drive to Memphis, fly to Raleigh, North Carolina, rent a car to drive about two hours to the funeral and then another two hours to her burial, and repeat the process coming back. With the amount of time they gave him, he would just be able to make the funeral if everything fell into place. There was no way he could go to the graveside. He asked if he could charter a plane at his own expense and have it fly right into Forrest City so he could make the services. He offered to pay for all of it, including Mr. Racine's salary. They declined his request, so he didn't go at all.

We held a service at 10:00 a.m. to coincide with her service in North Carolina. We even sung the same hymns that they would be singing at her service. The chapel was full of inmates, and several staff members even attended. He provided me the necessary information about his wife, and we conducted the service. There wasn't a dry eye in the place. He told me, "Coach, thank you! I will never forget this." Neither would we.

For the other inmates that died or their family members we held memorial services. These were less formal but just as moving and comforting. Any inmate was allowed to speak of the departed, and letters were written to the families and cards signed and passed on too. We told them things we loved and admired about the departed and all about the memorial service we held. It seemed to provide them some comfort and closure. Inevitably, we would get a return letter with specific questions that we always answered. The families were always grateful.

Attendance at these services was amazing every time. It was obvious we touched many more lives than we were aware of even in that place. Each story told seemed to amplify the importance of that man's life and all life. I didn't know each and every man personally, but there was always someone there who did.

The toughest were when the wives or children or parents or siblings of an inmate died. Rarely did an inmate get to actually go and attend the funeral. They were either denied or delayed or couldn't afford to pay for the officer that was required to escort them. I discovered it wasn't so much about what was said at these services that mattered; it was more about the willingness to gather and just have a presence with the suffering brother. The services were genuine expressions of love.

Chapter 57

Kara to Home Confinement

During the first week of August in 2010, Kara was finally released from the halfway house to home confinement. She would wear an ankle bracelet, but she would be home. As soon as that time expired, she would be free but still be on supervised release for five years. Being home meant family and friends and more freedom.

Kara bad been required to seek employment while at the halfway house until they sent her to a doctor and she was declared permanently disabled because of her muscular dystrophy. She would at least have to some income too. Under the terms of her supervised release, she would have to ask for permission to travel outside the state, but those requests were usually granted if she had a valid reason for going (like to see family).

Kara had to have a landline because of her ankle bracelet, so she had a phone. She also had a cell phone, which mean I could reach her if she was gone to the grocery store or anywhere else. She was settling in at Paul and Jen's and helping around the house as much as possible. The benefit of talking to each other daily had lifted both our spirits.

Carey, our son, was now working as a respiratory therapist for a local hospital home care, and he was taking time out to catch up with his mother. They went out to eat lunch and dinner and often to movies. The bonding was good for both of them. She was able to spend time with Mary Lynn also and our grandchildren. The oldest was now in college. The oldest boy had gotten his GED and was working at FedEx. The youngest boy was in high school, and Michelle, the youngest granddaughter, was in the sixth grade. They had really grown up fast. I was so proud of our family. Our children and grandchildren were carrying on without us, but I was the most proud of Kara, who had endured the greatest test of her life.

I don't think it is any surprise that as my spirit improved, so did my health. I was finished playing softball, but I was able to walk miles and felt much better. The medication they had given me had helped a great deal. However, the side effects of those medications had not yet shown up. They would, and pretty soon too.

Chapter 58

Kara Completely Free

Kara was released from the custody of the halfway house and the BOP on October 10, 2010. I spent the day weeping out of gratitude to God and relief she really was free.

We had also begun the process by filing paperwork for her to be allowed to come and visit me. From my end, it would be totally up to the warden, but it was not unusual for those requests to be granted. I filled out the proper paperwork and took it to my counselor, Mr. Racine. He said he saw no reason why the warden would deny it and promised he would rush it through.

Mr. Racine said, "Jack, I am going to walk these papers through to the warden myself. I will give him a summation of why I think he should approve your request. I think it will be okay with him. You deserve it, Jack."

I was so grateful because he didn't have to do that. However, he and I went back a long way. He had served as my counselor at the low following Mr. Gill's troubles back in 2003. He always knew he could count on me to obey the rules and not cause him any trouble. He knew I would stand up to the other inmates for what was right. He had taken me and other tutors to the training center to decorate for special events for the institution stuff. He had trusted us to be around his wife and children. I had a great relationship with Mr. Racine because he had always treated me fairly. Everything went smoothly on my end thanks to Mr. Racine.

It didn't go so smoothly for Kara on her end with her probation officer. Her probation officer told Kara she had real concerns about her visiting me. They were the following:

1. She absolutely couldn't leave the state for sixty days no matter what.
2. She was afraid I might ask Kara to bring in contraband.
3. And in so doing I would get Kara in trouble and cause her a great deal of unwanted paperwork.
4. She had no thing in writing from the prison that they didn't object.

After the warden had approved my visitation, I had to go back to Mr. Racine and ask for a letter stating it was okay for Kara to visit and mailed from the institution by him. He told me, "Jack, you type me up a letter, and I'll sign it and mail it to her. Just bring me her address." I wrote a two-page single-spaced letter stating that all the visits were carefully supervised and the institution had no worries at all about Kara coming to visit on any or all the available visitation days. I took the letter to Mr. Racine, and he signed it and placed it in the addressed envelope I had also provided. He made a copy of it all for me and told me to walk with him to the mail room, and he would send it off. I did, and the letter was sent.

Kara's probation officer received the letter, and she told Kara, "We'll talk about this when the sixty days are up." Kara's sixty days would be up on December 11. We would request a visit before Christmas. I wanted Kara to be with the family on Christmas. It fell on a Saturday that year. She needed to be home that day and not with me.

When Kara reported to the probation officer for her December report, she told Kara to put in a written request, and she would let her know. Kara requested that she be allowed to come visit on December 18, 2010. That was just two weeks away and only one week before Christmas. It was shaping up to be a memorable Christmas for both of us.

Chapter 59

Jack Preparing for Kara's Visit

I had continuously mentioned how much I was looking forward to Kara coming to visit me. I had talked about it for years. By the time she was released from custody on October 10, 2010, everyone, staff and inmates alike, knew I might be seeing her soon. They all seemed to be as excited as I was.

In my contemplative moments, I found myself thinking back. I remembered seeing Kara for the first time when I was four or five and she was two or three years old. My mom and her sister bad a beauty shop on Main Street in Rector, Arkansas. Kara's dad had a bakery. The stores were side by side and actually shared a common wall. The fire station was on one side of the building, next to the bakery, and there was a gravel road and railroad track on the other side of the building, next to the beauty shop. The two businesses were connected like a duplex.

I was just going to the beauty shop one afternoon, and I walked by the large windows that fronted the bakery. I saw what I thought was about a two-foot doll standing up front in the bakery right next to the window. I stopped and bent over to look at the doll. I stood there looking a good while. We were only about three feet apart with the window separating us. The doll was extremely fair-skinned and had great big blue eyes. The hair was really curly and reminded me of Shirley Temple and later of orphan Annie's hair. That was about the most lovely doll I had ever seen. I guess I stared at it for three or four minutes.

I went into the beauty shop. Mom didn't have a customer and was just up milling about straightening up her work area. She smiled at me when I came in and said, "Hi, Jack. What have you been up to?"

I climbed up in the beauty shop chair and said, "Mom, why does Mr. Pritchard have a doll in his window in the bakery? It is right up by the window."

Mom said, "Jack, I parked right in front of the bakery, and I didn't see a doll in Mr. Pritchard's window when I pulled up. Come on and show me."

I jumped up out of the chair and headed for the door with Mom right behind me. We walked out the door and down the sidewalk a few steps to the window with the doll. The doll was still there. I leaned down to look right in the doll's eyes and said, "See, Mom. Why's this doll in the window?"

Mom laughed. She said, "Jack, that's not a doll. That's Mr. Pritchard's daughter, Kara."

I still hadn't taken my eyes off the doll. I said, "No, Mom, I've stared at this doll for the longest, and it has not moved. It is a doll."

I had no sooner gotten the words out of my mouth when the doll suddenly blinked those big blue eyes. It was the first movement of any kind I had seen. It startled me so badly I jumped backward and stumbled into Mom, almost knocking her to the pavement.

Mom just roared with laugh ter. She said between gasps for air, "See, Jack. That is Mr. Pritchard's little girl, Kara." I looked closely at what I had thought all along was a doll. She just stared right back at me. I think I fell in love with that beautiful doll (Kara) that very day. I was older than her. I saw her almost daily but rarely interacted with her. She always seemed nearby and always seemed such a beautiful young lady.

I told her mom this story after we were married. Ms. Pritchard gave me an eight-inch-by-eleven-inch photo of her at that same age. It was black and white but still looked exactly like I remembered that doll that day so long ago. She still looked like a beautiful little doll to me.

I had other memories. Kara and I dating in high school. Two homecoming dances, two proms, ballgames (player-cheerleader), homecoming courts, birthdays, Christmases together, our marriage, fights and makeups, our children. I remembered the sacrifices made when I was in college and Kara's willingness later to uproot and move with me in my coaching career. In sickness and in health, rich or poor, for better or worse, in good times and bad, we always had each other. I still recalled the last time I saw her too. Walking away from me, handcuffed and being escorted by a US Marshal. I remember how badly I wanted her to just turn around so I could see her face one more time for just one brief moment. I had watched her turn the corner. She had never looked back. The pain was still so raw. It surprised me that way.

Chapter 60

Excitement Is Contagious

There was a man at the camp that faithfully served as the chapel clerk. His name was Rob Ruble. He was from St. Louis, Missouri. Rob and I drank coffee every morning together in my classroom before school started. Rob became an active member of the church. He was very bright with a contradictory background. He had worked in a union shop in an automobile factory and made a good living. He had also been a motorcycle club member, a drug addict, and an alcoholic. It had cost him his beautiful wife. He was also estranged from his son and daughter. However, more importantly, he was reformed.

A beautiful woman named Glenda from Perryville, Missouri, had heard of Rob from a man that prayed for his friend in Glenda's prayer group at her church. Eventually Glenda contacted Rob, and they began writing. She came to visit Rob every month at least once and often more. She became good friend with Rob's parents, and they often rode together for visits. They were all very close, and they visited on Saturday just like Paul visited me and usually at the same time. We had all met one another in the visiting room, and we became close friends, almost like family. Rob had told our story to his family, so they knew all about our circumstances.

When Rob's family and Glenda found out Kara was out, they were overjoyed. They were even happier when they found out she would be allowed to visit me once a month beginning in December 2010.

They had all discussed this at length, and they decided that when Kara was coming to visit me for the first time, they all wanted to be there to see the reunion. The visiting room opened at 8:00 a.m. and closed at 3:00 p.m. They usually arrived between 8:15 a.m. and 8:30 a.m. just like Paul. They decided they needed to be there by 7:00 a.m. so when the visitation room opened, they could be the first ones in at 8:00 a.m. in order to be in the room when Kara and I were reunited. That meant they would have to leave St. Louis around 2:00 a.m. in order to be there in time for our reunion.

As extraordinary as that seems, the entire camp began buzzing when they heard Kara was coming on December 18, 2010, to see me. Many of the inmates began trying to schedule their visits that same Saturday morning so they could glimpse our reunion. It became a big event for many of the inmates and their families.

The staff was equally excited. The officers that were actually working the visiting room that quarter began counting down the days with me when they saw me. Ms. Gill, Ms. Hill, Mr. Racine, and Chaplain Crosby all told me they would try to get by that day to see us and meet Kara. They did all show up as they said they would.

Chapter 61

December 18, 2010

Kara's probation officer finally made it official that Kara could come to visit on December 18, 2010. This was an answered prayer. One of my daily prayers for all this time had been that we would both live to see one another again. I was now fifty-nine. She was fifty-seven. It appeared we would, indeed, see each other again.

The week before the visit was excruciating. The clock seemed to be standing still. I was repeatedly told by inmates and staff alike that it might take us a few years to renew our relationship. Even my family members were warning that we had both changed. After all, they said, a great number of years had passed. I was warned to just be patient, and we would get to know each other again and be able to reestablish our relationship.

Friday night, December 17, 2010, was a sleepless night for me. I had prayed and prayed and thanked God and asked that he might keep them safe on their trip to the prison. Kara would be coming with Paul. At first, everyone in the family wanted to come, but it was rightly decided that no one would come so we could have some time together. I had already showered twice Friday night and even had my uniform ironed and pressed (something I never did with prison clothes).

So many inmates had come by wishing me the best with my visit. It had become a huge event. There was real excitement in the air. Many of the inmates said they would see me in the morning before my visit, and almost all of them said they wanted a full report after the visit on how it went.

Kara had bought new clothes, had her hair done, and even had a manicure. She was just as anxious and excited as I was. I later learned she had not slept much that Friday night either.

I was dressed and ready by 5:00 a.m. As soon as the count cleared (about 5:30 a.m.), I went to education to my classroom. I fixed a pot of coffee, and Rob joined me at about 6:15 a.m. We drank cup after cup and talked and talked. Rob was ready to call his family and to watch our reunion. He had called his parents and Glenda at 6:00 a.m. before he came to education as soon as the phones came on. They were right on schedule and only about an hour away from the institution. Rob went back to the dorm to dress properly for his visit.

After many of the inmates had come and gone, I walked alone up the sidewalk near the visiting room about 7:45 a.m. I was alone with my thoughts. I felt those same butterflies I used to get before a big ballgame when I knew I had a big role and would be tested. It was chilly outside, but my palms were sweating profusely. My mind wandered.

I had gone back to the last night Kara and I had been together. The night before our verdict had come in. The last night we had been intimate and had slept together. The last time we had been alone. That night was special, but we had been consumed with our fears and possibility of what might happen. That fear and worry had robbed us of the special time we had. We had not slept. We just held one another until the sun came up.

As I waited, I realized how much I did really love Kara and how badly I had missed her. It tore at my heart to think of all that time apart. I was getting way too emotional. As a result, I began to focus on how proud I was of Kara. We had lost so much. Time was more than seconds and minutes and hours and days and weeks and months and years. It was precious. Long sentences were handed out like it was just time! It wasn't that simple. Our justice system needed sentence reform. It is easy to say "Lock 'em up" when one doesn't really know and understand what it costs in relationships.

My mind flashed back over Kara. I couldn't relate much past my sixteenth birthday that didn't include Kara. She and I were really one. Our lives were so intertwined and had been for so long they could not be separated. I thought about our children and our grand-children and realized our oneness was generational. Because of the blessing of our children and our children's children, we would forever be thought of as one, Jack and Kara, Kara and Jack.

I was recalled from my recollection when the PA system roared, "Jack Phillips, 16286-076, Camp Ozark, report to visitation. Phillips, 16286-076, to visitation." The officer then added, "The day is finally here." I can't remember taking the thirty or forty steps to the door to the shakedown room. After the shakedown room, the next door would lead to the visitation room and to Kara.

Chapter 62

Reunited

There were two other men already in the shakedown room when I entered. They had given their ID cards to the officer, and he was writing down their names and numbers on his sign-in sheet. I knew he would then pat each man down, hand him his ID card, and tell him, "Enjoy your visit, and don't forget to give your ID to the officer at the desk." It was always the same routine. They would then open the door to the visitation room and see their visitors, and a huge smile would spread across their face. If there were young children, they would shout "Daddy!" and run and jump into their dad's arms. His eyes would fill with tears. I could tell the officer was delaying to get to me until the other men left.

As soon as they left the room, he locked the door to the visitation room and the door to the outside. We were absolutely alone. He did not want to be distracted. He said, "She's out there, Jack. I saw her. Man, I'm so happy for you. I've worked here eleven years, and this is the most excited I've ever been about an inmate's visit. I hope you have a great visit." He shook my hand.

I surprised and could only mumble a "Thank you" in return. I handed him my ID card, and he signed me in. When he was finished, I raised my arms above my head and turned around so he could pat me down.

He said, "Not today, Jack. I'm not patting you down going in or coming out. You open that door and go see your wife. You deserve it." He handed me my ID card.

I shook his hand again and thanked him. Well, the moment was here. It had been twelve years and thirteen days since we had laid eyes on each other. I couldn't wait to see Kara, but I had no idea how this would feel.

I opened the door and stopped. There was a large crowd around the officer's elevated station, where I would have to go to leave my ID card until my visit was over. That meant I would have to wait just a moment to begin my visit. I looked, and the closest person to me was my wife, Kara. There she stood with her back to me. It was the same view I had had the last time I bad seen her twelve years and thirteen years ago as she was being escorted away from me in hand-cuffs by a US Marshal. I was overcome with emotion as that thought crossed my mind. I was overcome again by how much I had wanted and needed her to just look back over her shoulder so I could see her face one more time. It was the strongest emotion I had ever felt. My knees could barely hold me up as I relived that long ago scene when she didn't look back.

At that very moment, at just the right time, just before I col-lapsed, she turned around. She turned her head and looked back over her shoulder. She saw me and smiled the biggest, most beautiful smile I would ever see in this lifetime. Oh, Kara!

That's all I had desperately wanted when I saw her last those many years before. All that heartache vanished in the face of that two-year-old doll who was now fifty-nine. She had looked back over her shoulder and smiled! It is all I had ever needed since I was a real little boy staring into the face of Mr. Pritchard's little girl, Kara. I had never really needed or wanted anything else. Just for Kara to look back and smile was perfect!

I rushed across the space between us and swept her up in my arms. The tears flowed easily and proudly. Nothing existed at that moment except Kara and me in that space. All outside noises, people, and distractions were just blotted out. There was twelve years and thirteen days in that sweet hug and the kiss that followed. The hug just lasted and lasted.

I heard someone clap and cheer, and then the entire visitation room erupted in clapping and cheering. Everyone was standing. Even the officers had stopped and stood up and were clapping and cheering. They even had tears in their eyes, as did everyone else. I handed the closest officer my ID card, and he shook my hand. The entire room continued cheering and clapping as Kara and I followed Paul to three empty seats. I waved and nodded my thanks to everyone in the room. When Kara and I sat down, everyone else in the room did too. Rob's parents and Rob and Glenda were in their familiar place over by the wall. They were all smiling and weeping and waving all at the same time. For the next twenty minutes or so, people got up and came over and congratulated us and introduced themselves to Kara.

It was almost like a resurrection would be. We had gone so long without seeing each other. It was very exciting and meaningful, more than either of us could have imagined or we could ever adequately express.

Postscript

All those who had predicted that Kara and I would have to get reacquainted were wrong. We didn't need any time to reconnect. We had never disconnected.

On July 27, 1970 (after three years of daring), we had been married. Over the years we had become one. Time and distance could never separate us, even "till death do us part."

We had talked and talked and talked the day of that first visit. We were finishing each other's sentences as if we had never been apart. We had gotten reacquainted that day with the tone of our voices and the tenor of our laughter. However, one look in Kara's eyes, one intimate look into each other's soul, had put everything back in place that had been disrupted twelve years and thirteen days ago.

That the first of twenty-one monthly visits that followed. Kara's supervised release was prematurely lifted after twenty-three months (instead of the sixty months she was sentenced to). God blessed us again. From then on, Kara could come visit every week. I could finally hug and kiss my wife and even sit and hold her hand. I would make my remaining time that much easier.

Our lives could now begin again after having been suspended for the really more than thirteen years since the fire on July 13, 1997. It was like coming out of a coma or a Rumpelstiltskin sleep. Our future was still obscured and hard to see, but at least we did have a future. The amazing thing was it still seemed bright.

The concept that Kara was *out* and *safe* would take a while to firmly set in my conscious mind. I kept finding myself worrying about her as if she were still in the system. I had ongoing nightmares about it, and I was also fearful she might inadvertently violate her supervised release. I wasn't worried about her purposely breaking a rule. I was more just worried she might break a rule unknowingly.

I was anxious to see her each week when she was released early from supervised release. Each night I called her and just listened to her voice and was so comforted and so thankful. It was the highlight of each day.

I did have a problem now with time. It seemed to slow down more and more in perfect accordance with my anxiousness to be home with Kara. I also seemed to have a mixed bag of emotions. I still had six years to do. I was going to miss a lot more time with her and the family even though she was out.

I was at the camp, which was good. I would be doing easy time. However, I would be sixty-six when released if I was released on my good time date of August 11, 2017, provided I lived. I hoped my physical health wouldn't fail me.

We had both had quite a spiritual experience. The role of inmate pastor at the Camp Church would challenge me and change me like nothing ever had. The Bible study and work in the church had the ability to change hundreds of men's lives. What I didn't know was the great spiritual leap I would make over the rest of my time incarcerated. I had much to learn and much more to experience. I would be the better man because of it.

My last days in prison and my spiritual journey through it all will be covered in the third book in this series. It is entitled *Ambassador in Chains: My Only Defense.*

About the Author

I am a retired schoolteacher. I have a BS in education with a double major in social studies / history. Also an MA in secondary education, administration and supervision. I taught high school for nineteen years and institutional GED for seventeen years. I created a math curriculum for GED called GED Math3 (GED math to the third power) and the book Teaching It Perfectly (TIP), an innovative way to teach writing skills and essay writing. I am a husband, father, grandfather, and great-grandfather. I am also a licensed minister of the Gospel.